"Done what?" Abby tried to sound forceful but knew she failed miserably. She'd never experienced real fear like this before, but then again, she'd never been married to a perfect stranger who seemed to know her better than any man ever had.

He reached out and she backed up until she met the wall behind her. Her pulse pounded, blood racing erratically. Anxiety held her paralyzed, but she had to admit feeling her first real frisson of excitement.

His thumb caressed her jawline, and his tone was steely. "You told me all about a woman who wore sexy lingerie, who drank champagne with her lover in a bubble bath while saxophone music echoed in the background. So tell me, Abby, how many times have you made love to the soulful sounds of a sax?"

Heated color rose to paint her cheeks. A fictitious lover on a nameless, sightless computer screen was one thing. Talking about her invented personality with her *husband* not more than six inches away was another thing entirely.

ABOUT THE AUTHOR

Once Kathy began researching Antarctica, its wildlife and its temporary residents, she became hooked on every aspect of that unique world. She was sorry to turn down a job offer there due to family and career commitments, but she hopes *Groom Unknown* will educate—as well as entertain—readers about this forgotten continent. Kathy lives in Colorado with her family.

Books by Kathy Clark

HARLEQUIN AMERICAN ROMANCE

333—SIGHT UNSEEN
348—PHANTOM ANGEL
366—ANGEL OF MERCY
383—STARTING OVER
428—GOOD MORNING, MISS GREENE
442—CODY'S LAST STAND
461—COUNT YOUR BLESSINGS
481—GOODBYE, DESPERADO

Kathy Clark

GROOM UNKNOWN

Harlequin Books

TORONTO • NEW YORK • LONDON
AMSTERDAM • PARIS • SYDNEY • HAMBURG
STOCKHOLM • ATHENS • TOKYO • MILAN
MADRID • WARSAW • BUDAPEST • AUCKLAND

To Bert . . . a great Antarctic explorer.

A special thanks to Kathy Loyd, Gwen Brodine and
Caron Connors who provided some fascinating
information on Antarctica that was invaluable to this book.

And to Jim, my favorite Hot Cop . . . make it happen!
You deserve the best. You're a very special friend.
Thanks, thanks, thanks
for everything.

ISBN 0-373-16536-6

GROOM UNKNOWN

Copyright © 1994 by Kathy Clark.

Chapter One

"Are you all right, Miss Harris?" the co-pilot asked. As Abigail's eyes focused on his green flight suit and two gold lieutenant's bars on his shoulder, she tried to sound casual.

"I'm fine, thanks."

"We're going to be landing in about forty-five minutes, and I thought you might need some time to change. The bathroom's too small to dress in, but you'll have all the privacy you need behind those boxes of supplies. The pilot and I will stay in the cockpit until you finish." The young man wiggled his fingers and winked. "That is, unless you need help. I'm good with zippers."

"I'll bet you are." Abigail smiled. She was flattered, but not fooled by his flirtation. After all, she was the only woman on this flight, and therefore the only woman on whom he could practice his charm. If her gorgeous older sister, Allison, or her vivacious younger sister, April, were here, the co-pilot wouldn't even have noticed Abby.

Usually that would have bothered her. But not today. Today was her wedding day, and she had an officer of her own waiting for her. "No thanks. I think I can handle everything alone," she told the young man.

But as she watched him walk away, a fresh attack of nerves rushed through her and she fumbled with the seat belt. In less than an hour she would meet and marry her dream lover. She could only hope that this impulse wouldn't turn out to be a nightmare.

She walked around the maze of boxes and mailbags until she found her garment bag hanging from an overhead compartment. Her fingers trembled as she unzipped the thick plastic and carefully took out the snow-white velvet wedding gown. It had caught her eye in a mall display window and had tempted her beyond resistance. Even though it had been on sale, it was the most expensive, ridiculously impractical dress she'd ever owned.

Although she thought of herself as average-looking, it was important to her that she be as attractive as possible when she and her fiancé first met. That was the thing that worried her most. He'd said her beauty was from within and that he didn't care what she looked like. But still, her feminine vanity didn't want him to be disappointed.

Oddly enough, it didn't matter to her whether or not he was handsome. She'd fallen in love with his personality, and she'd been completely honest in her arguments with herself that whether he looked like Mel Gibson or Danny DeVito was not important.

Abigail took off the blazer, silk blouse and tailored slacks she'd been wearing and neatly draped them over one of the boxes before opening her overnight case and touching up her makeup. She frowned at the dark circles beneath her tired blue eyes. Besides the sleeplessness her sudden decision had caused, the nineteen-hour trip from Los Angeles to New Zealand yesterday and the five additional hours to Antarctica were exhausting. And the thought of what might happen tonight—her wedding night— meant she wasn't likely to catch up on her sleep any time soon.

Actually, that prospect brought a shy smile to her lips. She knew him only by his code name, Lobo, but she also knew everything she needed to know. If he was as gentle and sweet and sexy as his notes, then he would be a wonderful lover. Anyone who knew the prim, proper Abigail Harris would be shocked, but it wasn't as if he was a complete stranger. She knew him from the inside out. She just hadn't had a chance to *see* that outside yet.

Her hands were still shaking, but now it was a combination of excitement and anticipation more than fear as she removed the gown from its hanger. She slipped the velvet, soft and sensual, over her head, and the dress slid down her body, encasing her feminine curves in pristine white. The rows of fake fur that bordered the round neckline and cuffs of the long sleeves tickled her skin. She had to struggle to pull the long zipper up the back of the gown, but she refused to call for help. Somehow she didn't think Lobo would approve of one of his junior officers seeing his bride's body before he did.

Meticulously she hung her other clothes in the garment bag, then retrieved her fur-lined boots from the canvas bag of clothing she'd been issued at the clothing distribution center in Christchurch late yesterday evening. She'd considered wearing high heels today, but when they'd told her the temperatures would be hovering a few degrees below freezing at the time of her landing, she'd decided to forgo fashion for practicality. She couldn't completely ignore her common sense.

When Abby opened her suitcase to pack her shoes, her gaze halted on the thick, three-ring binder she had tucked in next to the completely practical cotton panties she wore every day and the completely impractical negligee Allison had sent her as a wedding present. She took out the notebook, put the shoes into a plastic bag and refastened the suitcase. After removing the thick wool cape she had bought to match the gown, she rezipped the garment bag and returned to her seat. After draping the cape over the back of an empty seat, she sat and struggled to arrange the billowy skirt that filled not only all of the legroom between the seats, but poured out into the aisle, as well.

A glance out the window showed her that her destination wasn't yet in sight. Her hands lovingly caressed the black plastic cover of the thick notebook on her lap and she couldn't resist opening it.

There, printed out on hundreds of sheets of computer paper was the history of her romance with Lobo. When she'd joined the computer interaction service called CompuLink, she'd never dreamed it would connect her with the man of her dreams. In fact, all she'd been hoping for was some intelligent discussions with people interested in some of the same things she was.

But ever since that first evening when they'd begun exchanging notes, she'd been attracted to the man who went by the nickname of Lobo. He'd jumped into the middle of some speculation on the continental-drift theory, then had written to her private mailbox on the computer, expressing his agreement with her theories. He'd also told her he'd done research on the subject and hoped to get to Antarctica eventually for some on-site study.

Their messages to each other had been friendly but impersonal, at first. But even with those brief notes, there had been something special . . . something that made her look forward to the time she could spend on the computer with him. Abby slowly turned the pages, reliving the birth and development of her relationship with the mysterious Lobo.

July 7

A friend of mine was stationed in Antarctica a couple of years ago and he brought back what he thought was an interesting rock. It turned out to be a fossil of some sort of coniferous tree. He's drawn me a map where he found it so if I actually get to the Ice, I'll be able to see if I can find more. Of course, one small fossil isn't conclusive proof, but it's a beginning.

Sincerely,
Lobo

Yes, it was a beginning. Using the pseudonym Ladybug, she'd responded, expressing her interest in Antarctica and asking for more information about his own research on the subject. After that first evening, they'd spent hours sending messages back and forth across the telephone lines. With increasing eagerness, she read his words on her computer screen, then printed them out so she could save them and reread them later. Every day brought more notes and a budding awareness of the person behind the wild, wolfish nickname that seemed to fit him so well. And yet, she'd resisted knowing more.

July 31

Hi Ladybug,
Just got home from work and I'm exhausted. That group of people I'm working with are

denser than fog on the Mississippi. Anyway, I don't want to talk about them when I can talk to you. But you know, Ladybug, it would be nice to be able to put a face to a name. Actually, it would be nice to put a name to you. Tell me what you look like and what your real name is. You've kept me in suspense for almost a month....

> Curiously,
> Lobo

Abby understood his request, and even agreed with it to a certain extent. But she'd hesitated. It was so much more fun not to have to be plain, serious, dull Abigail. How could she explain to him that when she was writing to Lobo, she could be anyone she wanted to be? She could be beautiful, soft, feminine, talented and desirable—none of which she felt in real life.

Dear Lobo,

A little intrigue is good for the soul. I, too, wonder what you look like and where you live and all the other little details about you. But I like our relationship as it is. This way, we're getting to know each other from the inside out without being influenced by the color of our hair or the status of our jobs. And it's more romantic to dream about a mystery man named Lobo. Let's keep it this way, at least for a while.

> Ladybug

Either he agreed with her request or he was humoring her. But whichever, he continued writing to her—or rather to Ladybug. Not a day went by that they didn't exchange at least a half dozen notes. Abby found herself turning down other invitations and cutting her overtime to a minimum so she could hurry home from work and spend each evening with Lobo.

August 20

Dear Lobo,
    I've really enjoyed getting to know you during the past few weeks. It's amazing how my day no longer seems complete if there's not a message from you when I get home. And you never let me down. I always go to bed with a smile on my face lately.

                                              Ladybug

Dear Ladybug,
    Your last note sure made my mind wander from the personnel reports I'm working on tonight. Give me a chance someday and I'll really put a smile on your face when you go to bed!
                                              Lecherously,
                                              Lobo

They'd even spent Labor Day together, long distance, of course. They'd both missed their companies' picnics so they could share a long-distance picnic lunch of take-out chicken and potato salad. There was something special about that day that pushed them beyond mere friendship. It was the first day their relationship had ventured into something more intimate.

September 5

Dearest Ladybug,

I don't know what it is, but I feel especially close to you today. I don't know how it's possible to miss someone I've never met. But I do miss you. When I'm not writing to you or reading notes from you, I catch myself just sitting here, imagining what you look like. Sometimes I really hate that promise we made.

Logically, I understand that what we have is a special friendship and can go no further. But emotionally, I'm beginning to wish...

Lobo

Dearest Lobo,

Yes, I know exactly what you mean. But I guess we have to be grateful for what we've got instead of wishing for something that can never be.

Ladybug

Abby flipped through a few more pages that marked the passage of another month. As the autumn days began to cool, Lobo's and Ladybug's notes began to heat up.

October 1

My Sweet Ladybug,

I'm sitting here at my desk, looking outside at the moon and wishing you were here beside me. You've completely captured my thoughts. Now don't think I'm a complete loser, but I haven't gone on a date since you and I began writing. I guess I'm looking for someone special, like you....

Just seeing your name on my screen excites me. I want to touch you, taste you and make wild, passionate love to you by the light of the moon.

Oops, did I go too far? The last thing I want to do is to frighten you so much you'll run away.

Lovingly,
Lobo

I'm not running.

Ladybug

A shiver of anticipation trickled through her as she read more of their notes. Perhaps it was the anonymity or the fact that she felt very comfortable with him, but as his comments had become more sexually bold, she'd matched him, innuendo for innuendo, suggestion for suggestion, promise for promise.

October 15

Dearest Ladybug,

I was lying on my bed, thinking of you. I need you so much tonight. You have no idea what you do to me. If you were here, well, you can just imagine what condition I'm in right now. I want to take your clothes off piece by piece and taste every inch of your body. I want to feel you under me and feel myself inside you. I WANT YOU.

I know I promised, but it would mean so much to me if you would tell me your name and at least the color of your hair and eyes. I'll even start off this exchange of personal information by telling you that I'm a captain in the navy and move around working on special assignments. If you don't want to know more, stop reading now, but I'm 32 years old, healthy, over six feet tall, have blond hair and blue eyes and I'll even sign off, for the first time, with my real name.

Affectionately,
Prescott

Abby remembered the evening she'd received that note as clearly as if it was yesterday. She'd sat for almost an hour, considering the repercussions of this information. Before, Lobo's notes had been from a nameless, faceless man. But now she could almost picture him. And his name—such a wonderful name—was as uncommon and special as the man of her fantasies.

She battled with the dilemma, trying to decide if she should tell him about herself or if she should keep herself clothed in the protective robe of mystery. She didn't want to bore him with the uninteresting details of her life. Even her name wasn't exciting.

Finally she decided that since they would never meet, she would tell him about herself, with a few embellishments. What would it hurt since it would go no further than this? And she would start with a new name, a romantic name, one that inspired thoughts of adventure and passion. She paced around her small apartment and glanced at the books on her shelves. Scarlett? Cathy? Juliet? Her gaze dropped to her collection of videotapes. Maybe someone like Goldie or Julia or Cher or... Her attention focused on *Romancing the Stone*. Perfect. A story of romance *and* adventure. But Joan? That wasn't any better than Abigail. How about Angelina, the heroine in Joan Wilder's books. Yes, that had just the right sound. Sexy, exotic, beautiful. Not at all like the real Abigail.

Dearest Prescott,

I'll always think of you as Lobo, but I like the name Prescott. Okay, I'll tell you a little about myself. I'm thirty years old, have long black hair and blue eyes. I work for a research facility that doesn't allow me any freedom to perform my own studies. But it does pay the bills.

When I'm home, after exchanging my lab coat for a black lace teddy or maybe a silk robe (with NOTHING underneath!), I love to read, write poetry, listen to music, especially Kenny G, while I'm soaking in a bubble bath or trying out new recipes . . . or making mad, passionate love.

And my name is . . .

Angelina

Dearest Angelina,

You sound just as I'd pictured you. Tell me, my beautiful long-distance lover, who are you listening to Kenny G with? Is there a man in your life? As much as I hope there isn't, I want you to be happy. Ouch. It hurts to be so generous.

Jealously,
Prescott

That wasn't a difficult question to answer since even before she'd "met" Lobo, she hadn't dated much. Her work kept her busy, and the long hours in the BioGen lab had lessened her chances of meeting many eligible men.

Oh, there was a new guy, Bert, who was on some sort of special assignment at BioGen. He was tall, handsome and charming, just the type of man who made Abby feel most uncomfortable. Obviously accustomed to having women flock to him at the crook of his finger, Bert made his moves and Abby kept her distance. Even though she found herself occasionally sneaking a glance in his direction, and often catching him staring back at her, she'd resisted his offers of shared lunches or coffee after work.

Until three weeks ago. Finally he'd made her an offer she couldn't refuse. She'd agreed to go with him to a lecture about the hole in the ozone layer and predictions of the earth's future. Since it was more of a business meeting than a date, she'd been able to justify her acceptance.

But fate—and Lobo—had stepped in to change her life forever. She hadn't been able to make the date, which coincidentally was for this evening, and she hoped the note she'd sent him explained it clearly enough. No doubt he wouldn't have any trouble finding another willing female to accompany him.

And so, she'd been able in all good conscience to answer Prescott's question.

Dearest Prescott,
   No, there's no man in my life right now. My days consist of slaving over a hot Bunsen burner and my nights belong to you.

                                        Angelina

My sweet Angelina,
   Someone will come along to rescue you from

that lab sooner or later. Maybe a knight in a white dress naval uniform will drop by and sweep you off your feet like in the movie *An Officer and a Gentleman*.

> Gallantly,
> Prescott

Are you an officer and a gentleman?

> Angelina

Yes... and usually. It depends on the woman... and the size of the moon.

> Prescott

The pages sizzled beneath her fingers as she flipped through the two weeks that followed. But her hands stilled when she saw the exchange of notes that had forever changed the texture of her relationship with the man she still thought of as Lobo.

November 4

My sweet Angelina,

I've got some good news and some bad news. The commander of the naval support force in Antarctica had a heart attack and had to be transported out yesterday. He's going to be okay, but guess who was selected to take his place—me.

> Prescott

Congratulations. And the bad news is?

                                        Angelina

I'm leaving tomorrow morning and won't be back until the end of March or early April. But the really bad news is that there's no access to CompuLink there.

                                        Prescott

You mean we'll be out of touch for five months?

                                        Angelina

The only way around that would be for you to come with me.

                                        Prescott

Oh sure, I imagine the navy would love to have you bring along a "friend."

                                        Angelina

No, they wouldn't allow me to bring along a friend, but they wouldn't object if I brought along my wife, especially if she happens to be a very talented scientist.

                                        Prescott

Your *wife?*

                                        Angelina

Why not? I know it isn't logical or sensible. But you and I have been locked in a world of rigidity and restrictions all our lives. Maybe it's time we did something a little wild and unpredictable for a change.

I know we haven't actually mentioned the "L" word, but it's been evident in our notes for quite a while. Angelina, I've fallen in love with you.

Prescott

Yes, I feel the same, but this is so sudden. There are things we need to talk about.

Angelina

We'll have four months to talk and kiss and make love. Besides, not only will we be able to get to know each other better, but we can collaborate on our continental-drift research. Just think of the possibilities!

Prescott

What about my transportation, the license and all the other paperwork? It seems like so much to do in so little time.

Angelina

Just like a woman...thinking of the details. Well, you handle things on your end and I'll deal with things on mine. I'll arrange your transportation from Los Angeles to Antarctica. You'll have to spend the night in Christchurch, New Zealand and check in with headquarters there. They'll issue you all the cold-weather gear you'll need. And I'll get the marriage license and arrange for you to work in the lab at McMurdo Station.

All you have to do is quit your job, pack your Kenny G tapes and your sexy lingerie and I'll meet you wearing my dress whites and with the preacher standing beside me.

Picture me down on one knee in front of my computer, staring deeply into your eyes across the distance and asking—Sweet Angelina, will you marry me?

"MISS HARRIS, we're making our approach to Willie Field," the co-pilot informed her as he walked down the long aisle of the plane. He stopped suddenly, then exclaimed, "Wow...you look spectacular!"

Abby blushed at the compliment and tried to hide her discomfort by busily straightening the pages of her notebook and closing it. People had often commented on her intelligence or her outstanding grades or her meticulous attention to detail at work. But she didn't often hear compliments on her appearance. "Well, you know what they say about brides."

"Your fiancé must be a great guy, and one lucky fella. He sure won't have to worry about those long, cold nights.'' He smiled as he headed back to the cockpit.

Abby didn't know how to respond, so she turned her attention to the window. Her heart began pounding even more erratically at her first glimpse of the frozen continent as it appeared on the horizon. The crystal blue ocean below them was dotted with icebergs of all shapes and sizes. Ahead, she could see the snowcapped, rugged peaks of the mountains that shimmered like mounds of diamonds in the distance. The neatly arranged buildings of McMurdo Station looked like a small village that had been dropped into the middle of a white wilderness.

The plane began its descent and circled once before gliding to a landing on the runway that lay on the permanent ice shelf on top of McMurdo Sound. They taxied closer to a crowd of several hundred people who stood expectantly on the shoreline. For a moment, Abigail panicked as the realization struck that this would be her new home for the next four months and that she didn't know a single person out there.

Except for Prescott. Her dear Lobo.

When the plane stopped, the co-pilot stood and smiled down at her. "Good luck. I hope you have a happy marriage and enjoy summer on the Ice. Oh, and don't forget these.'' He picked up the bouquet of flowers she'd bought that morning on impulse before leaving Christchurch, and handed them to her.

She looked down at the wilted blossoms and limp leaves. They didn't look any better than she felt at the moment. "Thanks."

He gave her a jaunty wave, then returned to the front of the plane to help the pilot open the exit door and secure the stairway.

A blast of cold air rushed through the plane and Abigail reached for her cape. She swallowed back the nervous lump in her throat and stood. After returning her notebook to its place in her suitcase, she fluffed her hair, then proceeded to cover most of it up as she put on the heavy cape and pulled the fake-fur-lined hood onto her head.

It's not too late. You can still change your mind, a voice inside her head reminded her.

Of course it's too late. She's in love with the guy, another voice answered. *Besides, this is the adventure of a lifetime.*

Abby anxiously searched through the group of people, hoping to pick out the mysterious Lobo. She'd hoped she would somehow magically recognize him, but other than the fact that about half the crowd were wearing bright red parkas like the one she'd been issued and the other half were wearing military green ones, everyone looked similar. She didn't see any sign of a tall blond man in a white uniform. Maybe he had cold feet and was standing her up.

Cold feet! Of course, he'd have cold feet if he was standing out there on the ice. A near-hysterical giggle burst out and she swallowed it back. "Get a grip," she reprimanded herself. "You're on your way to a wedding—your own."

A whole new round of hows and whys arose to clutter her thoughts, but she pushed them aside. "This is right, this is right," she chanted, trying not to hyperventilate as she walked down the aisle toward the exit. As she stood at the top of the stairway, the frigid wind whipped around her, tugging at her full skirt and making her doubly glad she'd chosen to wear the boots and remembered to tuck a pair of gloves into the pocket of the cape.

The metal stairway stretched out of the front of the plane below the nose that rose upward to facilitate the unloading. Carefully, Abby descended the steps, forcing her weak knees to work.

She was nearing the bottom step when a man in a crisp white dress uniform beneath his open green parka separated from the crowd and stepped forward in long, strong strides. The brilliant sunlight sparkled off his golden blond hair and the gold stars and rows of colorful decorations on his chest. The pilot and co-pilot who had been lounging at the bottom of the stairway suddenly snapped to attention and saluted the approaching officer.

"Lobo?" Abigail whispered, visually approving his broad shoulders and tall, well-proportioned body even though she had yet to see his face.

He stopped and returned the salutes with sharp precision. Abigail held her breath as he slowly lifted his head, letting his gaze travel from the hemline of her gown, up the full skirt, over the fitted bodice and on to her face. His brilliant blue eyes widened in surprise, and Abigail felt her own jaw drop.

"Bert?" she gasped.

"Abigail!" he exclaimed simultaneously.

Chapter Two

"Lobo?"

"Angelina?"

"Bert?"

"Abigail?" he repeated in disbelief.

There must be some mistake. She couldn't be the woman who'd captured his heart, his fantasies, his future.

Prescott looked to the top of the airplane's metal stairway. It couldn't possibly be her. Then again, it couldn't possibly be anyone else, either. Only one woman would be exiting the plane in a wedding dress. And since there were no other passengers, logic made him conclude that she was his bride-to-be.

She stood there, nervously fingering the folds of the white cape. The noise of the crowd and the engine's cooling jets faded into oblivion. All he heard was the sound of his own pulse. Slowly, with one gloved hand curled around the railing, she descended the last few stairs. Judging by the expression on her face, Ange-

lina—Ladybug—no, Abigail, was just as shocked as
he was.

An odd mixture of emotions surged through him.
Surprise, disappointment, anger and a hint of excitement. A burst of wind swirled around them, billow-
ing her skirts and tugging the hood off her head. She
wore her dark hair long and loose, unlike the severe
twist she'd always kept it styled in for the lab. The
blazing Antarctic sun glinted off the thick, curling
strands, showing a hint of red that he'd never noticed under the harsh glare of the office's fluorescent
lighting.

His attention moved to her eyes—wide, midnight
blue pools—too dark to read and yet too compelling
to ignore. They were such an unusual color and
framed by the longest, thickest lashes he'd ever seen.
Funny he'd never noticed that, either.

Her lips—full, deliciously moist and naturally
rosy—were parted as if she couldn't quite voice her
thoughts. Her face was flushed, particularly her high
cheekbones. Whether it was a result of cosmetics or
their impending meeting, he couldn't say. But it con-
trasted strikingly with the pale perfection of the rest
of her skin.

Prescott sucked a breath as deeply into his lungs as
the thin, cold air allowed. Most of all, what he'd
never noticed until this moment was how incredibly
beautiful she was. At home, she'd faded into the
background, content to let her work speak for her.
But gone was the lab coat. Gone were the tweed pants

and neutral-colored blouses. And definitely gone were the glasses that hid the Mediterranean blue of her eyes. This was the sweet Angelina he'd fallen in love with.

Yet she was the same Abigail who'd carelessly crushed whatever relationship might have developed between them. In spite of her lack of encouragement and his own better judgment, he'd been attracted to her. He knew he had a job to do that didn't include dating other employees. But he might as well have spared himself the energy because every time they'd had a chance to get closer, she'd shut him out with a cool glance or a pointed comment about their project. She'd rejected him without a second thought, except for one date that had never happened.

And now he was going to marry her—Angelina, the warm, vivacious, intelligent woman he'd fallen for... or maybe it was Abigail, the medical genius who had no thoughts for anything but her work. He resisted the urge to look around and see if someone was filming this for "America's Funniest Home Videos" because this was the most unlikely turn of events imaginable. He would never in a million years have guessed that the hot-blooded Angelina and the cold-blooded Abigail were one and the same person.

She paused on the last step, the difference in heights bringing them about eye level. For several seconds, her gaze locked with his...searching. For what? Reassurance? Devotion? Answers? Well, he didn't have any of those. He was as confused about this whole situation as she was.

And as much as he wanted to offer reassurance and devotion, he couldn't, not unconditionally. She had a lot of explaining to do. But definitely not in front of a couple hundred people. In the months ahead, with days of all sun and no moon, she'd have plenty of time to talk.

Good manners, if nothing else, forced him to step forward across those last frozen inches to claim the hand of his intended wife. "Welcome to the bottom of the world..." He hesitated, not sure what name he should call her. Somehow, looking as different as she did, he couldn't call her Abigail. And yet he couldn't bring himself to call her his Angelina, either. "...Abby," he finished, settling on a compromise until he could get to the bottom of this name confusion.

She took the final step that readjusted their heights so that she was looking up at him. Though she wasn't small for a woman, he dwarfed her. A strange sensation of protectiveness surged inside him. Despite their differences, she would be his wife, his responsibility. And Captain Prescott Roberts took his obligations seriously.

"Lobo?" Her voice was still filled with incredulity and her touch was tentative as she took his hand.

"That's me," he answered. Though the summer day was warm by Antarctic standards, her breath hung suspended in the air between them. "I trust you had a good flight."

She nodded, not seeming to know what else to say.

He became aware of the crowd's murmured speculation behind him. Weddings at the isolated station, while not unheard of, were definitely rare and certainly a cause for celebration among all the residents. Any excuse for a party, he'd learned during his short time here.

Beside him, Reverend Leland cleared his throat.

"I promised I'd be waiting with a man of the cloth," Prescott said, watching her for a reaction. Now that she was here, would she change her mind and leave him at the altar with a wedding ring burning in his jacket pocket?

She was silent for a few seconds, and Prescott was beginning to believe she was going to refuse to marry him. Not that it really mattered if she did call it off. His pride would be damaged, but people would understand. And yet... As another gust of wind teased her hair, sending it tumbling in shiny curls over one shoulder, he couldn't resist reaching out and touching it. He buried his fingers in its thickness, and her wide, guarded eyes softened as his knuckles brushed her cheek.

Her fragrance, lightly floral and feminine, filled his nostrils, and he remembered the many times they'd worked side by side in the lab and that same fresh, tantalizing smell had sent his hormones raging. It had all been so unintentionally provocative on her part that he'd never mentioned it. But he'd spent several long, restless nights alone in his bed thinking of how that petite body would feel beneath his. That is, until he'd met Ladybug and turned his attentions to her.

She'd filled his thoughts, his dreams, his longings until there wasn't room for anyone else. And now he'd discovered that the two women who had tormented his peace of mind for the past few months were one and the same. Reluctantly he admitted to himself that it did matter whether or not she chose to stay. He wanted her . . . whoever she was.

"Not getting cold feet are you?" he asked softly, his words for her ears only.

"No," she snapped back, the familiar coolness rushing into her eyes again. "Not unless you don't want to marry me anymore."

With a flash of insight, he realized she didn't want to be left alone at the altar any more than he did. "I still want to marry you, Abby."

Her guard dropped slightly and her lips curved into a shy smile, one he couldn't help returning. She was gorgeous. She was his.

Prescott's fingers tightened around her much smaller hand, and he lifted it to his lips as he gave her a courtly bow. The crowd behind him cheered their encouragement.

Prescott addressed the co-pilot. "Take care of the lady's bags, please. You can leave them in my room," he added, tossing the lower-ranked officer his keys.

"Yes, sir!" the young man responded and saluted again.

As if by plan, the group swarmed around them and provided an excited escort from the runway, down the main street and to the galley. Prescott opened the door and held it as Abby preceded him inside.

They passed through the large coatroom where everyone removed their outerwear and hung it on hooks that lined the walls. As they walked into the main mess hall, the warmth of the huge room—used for everything from lectures to dances to their three daily meals—engulfed them. The committee of party planners had done a good job, he realized. While he'd been working and waiting this morning, they'd transformed the plain, military-style room into a wedding chapel and reception hall.

Bells, made from white crepe paper, hung from the ceiling. Rows of chairs had been set up, facing an arch of silk flowers and an altar at the front of the room. Even a cake with four slightly askew tiers had been baked and now grandly served as a centerpiece on a lace-covered table. Prescott accepted the cake's appearance as a minor miracle. In his experience, the kitchen could barely produce an edible meal, let alone a beautifully decorated cake. Still, he refused to question anything. This was his wedding day, and he was glad it would be special for Angelina…and Abby.

"I hadn't expected all this," Abby said as she unfastened her cape.

"Neither had I," Prescott admitted. "The party committee did a great job."

"Party committee?"

"Things are a lot different down here, as you'll soon find out. None of what you've heard about the starkness and isolation of Antarctica was an exaggeration. We make our own entertainment here." Even as he said the words, he recognized a double entendre in them.

Evidently so did she. She flushed becomingly, the color heightening in her cheeks.

The minister cleared his throat.

Prescott had arranged for a young couple to stand up with them. The wife, a short, cheerful woman with a bubbly demeanor, hurried over to Abby. "Hi, I'm Sandy and that handsome lieutenant commander over by the punch bowl is my husband, Bill."

"Pleased to meet you," Abby said with a gracious smile, and Prescott wondered what it would feel like to be the recipient of that warmth. At work, she'd rarely smiled. Which, as it turned out, was probably a good thing because he felt his knees weaken at the sight.

"Captain Roberts has been looking forward to your arrival," Sandy added. "Last night, some of the guys threw him a bachelor party, but he was so anxious about your flight today that he didn't even stay out late."

"Thanks for the detailed report," Prescott said dryly. "You know officers are never nervous about anything. At least we wouldn't admit it."

"Oh, you military men are all the same," Sandy sputtered. "You plan the conquest of a woman's heart with the same precision as an assault in Desert Storm."

"Well, that's not exactly true in this case—" Prescott started to explain, but was interrupted when Bill strode over and slapped him on the back.

"The sooner you get this over with, the sooner you can start your honeymoon." Bill's eyebrows rose expressively.

The color drained from Abby's face. Somehow, in their correspondence, a mad affair had sounded incredibly sensuous. They'd both been bold and articulate about what they'd do when they found their first moment of privacy. Now that he stood next to the woman he knew as the frigid Abigail, their possible intimacy was colored by an added dimension.

He'd been anxious to meet Angelina, and had every intention of claiming her physically, the same way he'd claimed her emotionally through the computer. But Abigail was a different story. Never could he imagine Abigail Harris, in bed or anywhere else, joining him with wild abandon. The images didn't jibe.

"So what do you say?" Bill demanded. "You gonna let her make an honest man out of you?"

"Stop," Sandy said, punching her husband playfully on the arm. "When we got married you were a nervous wreck."

"Not me," he protested. "I was totally cool."

"So why did the best man stand behind you? Wasn't it so you wouldn't hit the ground if you passed out?"

"I'd just returned from six months at sea," he explained with a snort. "I hadn't gotten my land legs yet."

Prescott noticed Reverend Leland walk to the front of the room and motion for the ceremony to begin. Those residents who wanted to witness the wedding or who simply wanted to party had filed through the door and taken their seats.

"Oh, I almost forgot," Prescott said as he turned back to a very silent Abby. He took away the brown, withered blossoms she still held and handed her the pink and white silk flowers one of his clerks had obtained for the occasion.

Sandy smiled at Abby. "Don't forget, something old and something new. Well, here's something borrowed and something blue. It's okay to double up on them on such short notice." She slipped a blue topaz ring off her finger and handed it to Abby. "This belonged to my grandmother and she was married for sixty-two years, so it should bring good luck."

"Thanks," Abby said. "I think we're going to need all the good luck we can get."

Prescott listened for any hint of sarcasm in her tone, but found none. She seemed to be genuinely anxious for this marriage to work.

"Just make the captain happy," Sandy replied. "He's a nice guy."

For a few seconds, Prescott's gaze held Abby's. He noticed her lips were trembling and he was seized by a sudden urge to reassure her with a tender kiss. Captain Prescott Roberts usually didn't have such thoughts; at least he hadn't for a very long time. For the past dozen years he'd been focusing on his career. Juggling full-time military duty with working toward his Ph.D. hadn't left much energy for frivolous distractions.

Abigail had reawakened those desires, but corresponding with Angelina had made them go wild. She'd managed to uncover an aspect of his personality he'd forgotten existed. Could Abby do the same?

More importantly, would she want to?

Angelina wouldn't object if he rubbed his thumb gently across those delicious-looking lips. Abigail would likely give him that reprimanding look that could freeze Phoenix.

What the hell had he gotten himself into?

"You and Bill go on up there," Sandy said, sensing someone needed to take control and easily stepping into the role. She wrapped her arm around Abby's shoulders and began pulling her to the back of the room. "When the piano player starts the wedding march, we'll walk down the aisle. You guys just stand up there and look gorgeous."

"Piano player?" Abby asked.

"We don't have an organ, so we improvise," Sandy explained.

"It's not too late to turn tail and run," Prescott whispered into Abby's ear, softly taunting. But his tease backfired as her soft hair tickled his lips and brought an immediate response to his eager loins.

She looked at him, a hint of defiance spiking her eyes. "I made a commitment. I keep my word."

"Is that Abigail's word or Angelina's?" he asked with just a touch of sarcasm.

"Who wants to know...Bert or Lobo?" she retorted, tilting her chin to show she wasn't going meekly into this union. Nor would she give him the home-court advantage.

"What is it with you two?" Bill demanded. "Twenty minutes ago the captain was pacing the halls demanding to know if your plane had landed yet or if there was any word from you."

Abby looked at Prescott in surprise, seeming to draw strength from Bill's words.

"Go," Sandy said, shooing the men toward the minister. "We're just going to step into the hall and fix Abby's dress."

The door swished to a halt behind the two women.

"It's not a death sentence," Bill said.

Right now, Prescott didn't know if he was annoyed or challenged by Abby's attitude. But he, too, was a man of his word. In a moment of weakness, or something else, he'd decided he wanted Angelina in his life, in his bed, forever. He'd issued the proposal, even forming letters on the screen in the shape of a heart.

He remembered anxiously waiting for her answer, succumbing to the urge to yell "Yes!" when the answer had been in the affirmative. Suddenly, the magnitude of that moment loomed large. Forever was a very long time.

"I'm sure it's just prewedding jitters. Everybody has them," Bill commented encouragingly.

Prescott nodded in distraction. Oblivious to the hundred or so people around him, he walked with Bill to the front of the room where they joined the minister. The man nodded, and the piano player began a rousing version of the wedding march.

Prescott's heart skipped a couple of beats. The door opened and Sandy and Abby walked through, his future bride clutching the flowers in her hands. Sandy smiled reassuringly at Abby, then began the slow walk down the aisle while Abby waited at the back of the room.

But he didn't watch the maid of honor. Instead, his gaze was riveted on Abby. She had discarded her cape and gloves. The tangles had been combed from her hair so that it flowed around her shoulders in a thick mass, its darkness made more vivid as it lay against the stark whiteness of her wedding gown. Her eyes were open wide, a hint of something that might have been fear unsuccessfully hiding there.

Sandy halted on the other side of the minister and turned to look at the bride. The roomful of guests stood and watched as Abby moved toward him. Her gaze sought out Prescott's. She didn't glance around, merely looked at him as she stepped forward in time to the music.

When the final chord was struck, the silence was almost tangible.

"Please join hands," Reverend Leland prompted.

Abby, her knuckles white from the grip, unwrapped a hand from the stems of the silk flowers and handed the bouquet to Sandy. Her bare hand slipped into his grasp as if made for that very purpose. Prescott squeezed gently, offering the physical reassurance he was unable to voice.

"Dearly beloved," the minister began. "We have gathered here to unite Angelina—"

"Uh . . . it's not Angelina," Abby whispered, leaning toward the minister.

He looked confused, but reached into the pocket of his suit and pulled out a pen. "Okay, then what is the name you want on your marriage certificate?"

"Abigail Jane Harris," she answered, then leaned back after casting Prescott an apologetic look.

Again speaking loudly enough for the crowd to hear, the minister began again. "Dearly beloved, we have gathered here to unite Abigail Jane Harris and Prescott William Roberts..."

"Where did the Bert come from?" Abby leaned toward Prescott and whispered.

"Bert?" the minister echoed.

"It's a long story. I'll tell you later," Prescott answered softly.

Reverend Leland gave them both a severe look and continued with the ceremony, "...in the bonds of holy matrimony."

If possible, her hand grew even colder. And as if from a great distance, he heard the clergyman's voice, followed by Abby, shyly, softly saying "I do." Then she turned to him, looking up at him through those indecently long eyelashes. The overhead lighting gave her eyes the luminescent quality of the deep blue ocean sparkling beneath a shelf of crystal-clear ice.

For a flash of time he felt his heart melt. She looked so small and vulnerable. Yet the next moment came a burst of frustration, mingled with anger, for the callous way she'd treated Bert, then agreed to marry a person without so much as having seen his face. He wasn't too crazy about her decision-making process, especially since he and Bert were one and the same person...sort of. No, it wasn't too late. He could still call this whole farce off.

But when Reverend Leland looked at him and nodded, he heard his own voice say "I do."

She took off the ring she'd been wearing on her thumb. He hadn't really expected to receive a wedding band, and the fact she'd thought of it touched him. "With this ring, I thee wed," she said softly, her hands shaking as she tried to force the band over his knuckle.

Their gazes met. Hers was unreadable, but there was a shimmer that looked suspiciously like tears glistening in her darkened eyes. The gold band settled on his finger, its metal warm from being on Abby's thumb. He stared at it, watching the way the light glinted off the polished gold. A symbol of never-ending love the words of the service went. But it was more than that, Prescott realized, much more.

"Captain Roberts," the minister prompted.

Prescott fished inside his dress uniform jacket for the box containing the ring he'd so carefully selected before leaving Boulder. He'd sprung for a two-carat marquise-cut diamond, ignoring the cost. He and Abby didn't have the huge expenses associated with a big wedding and honeymoon, so he could afford to splurge a little. Besides, he was only going to get married once. Right?

He pulled the ring from the box and noticed it was much colder than the one warmed by her touch. With a single motion, he slid the ring onto her finger, amazed at the perfect fit. As if it was an omen.

"You may kiss the bride."

That was something he'd imagined doing to both of the women in his life.

He noticed her breathing in shallow bursts, her chest rising and falling rapidly. With one hand, he placed his palm against the small of her back, flesh against velvet. Using the other, he captured her chin. Slowly he lowered his head toward her.

Nervously she licked her lower lip and the sight of her pink tongue sent an odd burst of desire through him. With this single kiss, she'd be his before man and God.

He touched his lips to hers, tasting, exploring. She smelled sweet, of perfume and promises. Her mouth was inviting, leaving him hungry for more.

But before it really began, it was over.

Bill slapped him on the back and Sandy offered her teary congratulations. The spectators stood and applauded as the bride and groom made their way up the aisle.

"A toast," Bill called. Somehow, a bottle of champagne found its way into his hands. He popped the cork, letting the contents rush out and bubble down the sides. Sandy used two kitchen-issue cut-glass goblets to try to capture the overflowing sparkling wine, then handed them to the silent couple. Within a minute, several bottles had been opened and people were looking toward Prescott, their glasses full and waiting for his toast.

He was comfortable being in command, but didn't care for being the object of this kind of attention.

"Okay," Bill said, stepping forward. "As best man, I'll propose the toast." Prescott had never felt more relieved in his entire life. "To the newlyweds. May you find happiness together." He raised his glass in Abby and Prescott's direction. "And since you'll have someone to keep you warm at night, may you never have cold feet again!"

Prescott frowned at Bill, but was unable to say anything since a chorus of "Hear! Hear!" went through the crowd.

"Your turn," Bill said, not-so-gently nudging his commanding officer.

Faced with the expectant looks of over a hundred people, Prescott couldn't refuse. "To my bride," he said, inclining the glass in her direction. "I hope we'll always be as happy as we've been the last few months."

"Go on, Abby," Sandy encouraged.

A becoming blush painted Abby's cheeks, making him notice just how pale she was. If this ceremony was a strain on him, it was equally stressful for her. She started, then stopped, clearing her throat nervously. "To the future," she said quietly.

Abby and Prescott toasted each other, the clink of inexpensive glass filling the silence.

"We need a picture," Bill said, putting down his drink and grabbing a small camera from the table. "Of course, you'll probably have children before we get off the Ice to get the film developed."

All hint of color vanished from Abby's face.

"Link your arms together," Sandy urged. "You know, the traditional pose."

They did, but the maneuver was awkward because of their height difference. Prescott spilled too much champagne into her mouth when he bumped her elbow. But Abby gulped gamely and swallowed it all. People cheered and the camera flashed.

"You okay?" he asked, grabbing a napkin and handing it to her.

"I don't suppose there are any dry cleaners nearby."

He dabbed a drop of the amber-colored liquid from her dress, then realized just how close he was to her breasts. He froze. His action was naturally intimate—the action of a husband toward a wife, not a man toward a woman he hardly knew. He looked at her, reading the same confusion and awkwardness in her expression. "I'm sorry," Prescott said. "Maybe you should do this yourself."

"Yes," she agreed, taking the napkin from him. The movement made her diamond glitter, a not-so-subtle reminder that they were married, even if it felt like a sham. From the back of the room, music filled the air, from a cassette that was obviously well past its prime. "I think they're waiting for us to start the first dance," Abby said.

For months, he'd dreamed of having Angelina in his arms, the softness of her breasts pressed against the hardness of his chest. He'd imagined the scent of her filling his senses. He'd imagined her hair feathering across him.

And now that the opportunity had arrived, he wanted to demand an end to the farce, to know why she'd callously rejected him when he was Bert before flying off to marry a man she'd never met. And he wanted to know why she'd lied to him about her name and God knows what else. A fresh wave of anger surged through him.

"Shall we?" he offered. Though he truly didn't want to dance with her until she'd had time to explain a few things, he didn't want to make a scene, either. After all, only a few hours ago, he'd been anxious to meet the woman with whom he intended to share the rest of his life. He extended his hand and she took it.

The song was an oldie, a slow one he remembered from his high school prom. He took Abby in his arms, surprised at how natural the position felt—as if she was made to fit into his arms. "You could smile," he told his bride as they began moving around the floor.

"Why? You don't seem any more pleased about this than I am."

"I don't think we should discuss that right now. I just don't want to disappoint all my friends who've gone out of their way to provide a wonderful wedding and reception for us, despite limited resources. There'll be plenty of time for us to talk tonight. In our room."

"*Our* room?"

"We're married, Abby. Surely you didn't expect his-and-her bedrooms?"

"No," she said. "But I didn't expect to meet *you* down here, either."

"I think we've established we were both a little surprised by the discovery."

Other couples joined them on the dance floor, and he had to move quickly to avoid being jostled.

"Surprised is an understatement."

"Agreed," he said, subtly inhaling the scent of her.

"But after all this, we can't possibly live together as husband and wife," she said, words running together in a rush.

"Why not? We were married legally. Most married couples sleep together on their honeymoon."

"But we're not most couples," Abby protested. "We hardly know each other."

"You're right about that," he said, knowing a touch of bitterness tinged his words. "I thought I knew you, Angelina. At the beginning of our correspondence, you promised you'd always be open and honest with me."

She looked up, eyes angry. "And I thought I knew you, Captain Lobo Bert Prescott Roberts."

The Abigail at work was always serious and unemotional. The sweet lady he'd met over a computer linkup was always teasing and sensual. But the Abby in his arms was completely different from either. This one could give as well as she got, be fiery and sarcastic. What the hell had he gotten himself into? he wondered for the hundredth time in as many minutes.

The music ended and the crowd made a circle around them, evidently ready to socialize with them.

"This isn't the time, or the place," he said. "Let's go to our room." She didn't object, so he placed his hand at the small of the back, guiding her toward the door. Bill and Sandy hurried over.

"Wait," Bill said. "I know you're anxious to get your wife alone, but we've got wedding presents. You can't escape yet."

Abby looked at him, but Prescott had no option but to agree. Bill handed him another bottle of champagne, while Sandy gave Abby a box wrapped in six-month-old newspaper. "Open it," Sandy urged.

Abby did and gingerly lifted a sexy red teddy from the box. Heated color washed across her face once again. Men called out bawdy comments and Prescott had to force back the urge to issue a military-style command to shut them all up. After all, they were only trying to have a little fun on a barren continent where diversion was in short supply.

For the next half hour as they opened more gifts, both Abby and Prescott endured some good-natured ribbing about the night ahead. An image, hot and vivid, of how she'd look in the frothy lingerie assaulted his starved senses. The Angelina he'd met via modem was made for red lace and satin ribbon. The richness of the color would emphasize the creamy softness of her skin and complement the darkness of her hair.

A knot twisted somewhere in the region of his gut. He'd been ready for her for so long. And she'd said she was ready for him. But the expression in her eyes now gave question to the words she'd entered on her computer screen. Through tight lips, he thanked everyone.

"We'll try to save some hot water for you," Sandy said, outrageously winking at Abby. "You'll probably need a nice long bath in the morning to help ease sore muscles, if you know what I mean."

Prescott and Abby left, carrying their packages. He helped her into her cape, then held open the door leading to the outside. "It's going to be odd living in daylight around the clock," she said, her warm breath freezing on the frigid air. "I wonder if I'll get used to it."

"The nights and days sort of run together here," he responded automatically. Such a silly conversation for two newlyweds, he thought, but couldn't think of anything better to discuss.

The rest of the walk to his dorm room in the officers' quarters was accomplished in a silence impossible in any other part of the world. Here there were few birds and virtually no sounds from aircraft or vehicles. At the bottom of the world, they were almost completely cut off from civilization as they had known it. As he'd already learned, personalities, away from conventional rules and regulations, were radically different. Relationships were intense and usually brief, passions hot in contrast to the bone-numbing cold. He'd also learned that success rates of relationships once off the Ice were in the five percent range. Not good odds, particularly considering the way his and Abby's had started.

They entered the hallway and walked to the end room, then paused outside the door. With a hand on the knob, the ambivalent groom announced, "Well, Mrs. Roberts, we're home."

Chapter Three

Abigail looked up into the arctic blue depths of her husband's eyes.

Her husband.

The words stuck in her mind, playing themselves over and over again. He stood patiently in the doorway, waiting for her to enter the ridiculously small room. There was a teasing gleam in his eye as if he was trying to decide whether or not to sweep her into his arms and carry her over the threshold.

Abigail's emotions were mixed at the thought. After the farce of their wedding, to partake of the traditional beginning of a honeymoon seemed a desecration. But then there was a niggling desire to feel herself being lifted into his powerful arms and snuggled against his broad chest. How strange that she'd never noticed how tall and well proportioned Bert was before today.

So, big deal, he has a nice body, she thought to herself. That certainly doesn't mean he's going to make a good husband. On the other hand, it should make her visit to Antarctica an exciting one, even if the marriage didn't last!

Abigail was immediately ashamed at that thought. No one should go into a marriage with the idea that it isn't going to last. She had to put forth a little effort, at least, to see if things were worth salvaging.

Taking the decision out of Bert's hands, she stepped around him and entered the room. Pausing just inside, she surveyed her new home. So this was where she'd spend the next four months with Lobo—Captain Roberts—her husband, day and night. The man was turning out to have more personalities than Sybil.

He stepped in behind her, but wasn't ready for her abrupt stop. "Sorry," she mumbled automatically as he bumped into her. Bert said nothing, but she was very aware that he didn't move away. Although he wasn't touching her, she felt the heat radiating from his body and inhaled his spicy, masculine after-shave. The door clicked ominously behind them, sealing them in remote silence, a silence unlike any she'd ever experienced before.

Abigail wanted to skitter across the room, but she forced herself to calmly step away, moving slowly as if the Spartan decor was the most interesting sight on earth. She noticed that her luggage had been delivered. The fact that her belongings, along with the two large canvas bags that held her cold-weather gear, rested on the end of the double bed made the entire living situation seem more permanent.

"I'm sure it's not what you're used to," Bert said.

She looked at him, startled. That was not at all what she'd expected him to say the minute they had some privacy. Warily, she put the width of the bed between them, all the while watching his expression, which was as hostile as the frozen environment. "It's fine," she answered, wondering when they'd get to the *real* topic foremost on both of their minds.

"At least you can be sure no one will jog past your window at five o'clock in the morning." He walked over to the curtain and lifted it. "No window. It's one of the tricks in learning how to deal with the differences here. Some people paint murals on their walls, some hang pictures, while others pretend there's a window and hang curtains."

"Considering there's not much variety in the landscape and that it never gets dark here during the summer, I can't imagine why anyone would want a window, even a make-believe one."

One light brown eyebrow cocked as he drawled, "A person's imagination can be a powerful thing, you know."

His sarcasm wasn't wasted on her. But it made her consider the situation from a whole different perspective. So far she'd thought only of how he'd deceived her. Now she realized he was probably very disappointed in his bride. It was likely that his own imagination had created a tall, gorgeous female like her sister Allison, sitting at the other end of his modem. What a shock it must have been to find it was just plain old Abigail.

As all the self-confidence that had been building the past few months drained away, Abigail was suddenly aware of how exhausted she was. It seemed like she'd been flying for days, and what little sleep she'd been getting hadn't been restful because she'd been so caught up in planning her wedding and the trip to Antarctica.

When she realized her gaze was focused longingly on the bed, she looked up and saw that Bert was watching her with an expression that could have been excitement, or even worse, amusement. *Oh great, now he thinks you're dying to jump into bed with him.*

"Yes, we're really lucky to get a double bed," Bert commented, doing nothing to dispel her discomfort. "Most of the rooms have singles, but I heard that one of the other officers brought his wife along a few years ago and he skuaed this bed from somewhere."

"Skuaed?"

"It's a slang word you'll hear a lot around here," he explained with a hint of a smile. "A skua is a type of gull that is a renowned scavenger. Whenever someone has something they don't need any longer, they put it in a skua pile, and whoever needs it, takes it. Or when someone leaves, whatever they can't take with them is skuaed by the next crew." He glanced around the room and motioned to two mismatched chest of drawers. "These came from the pile, too. My stuff is in the one by the door, so you can stow your things in this one." He indicated a six-drawer chest next to a large wardrobe. "And I left some space for you in there, as well."

"Thanks." Abigail yawned and made little effort to hide it. In fact, she exaggerated it in hopes he would leave so she could have a chance to think things through and consider all her options.

He began unfastening the bright polished brass buttons of his jacket. "It *is* getting late, isn't it? I guess we'd better get ready for bed."

As much as she wanted to turn away, her attention was riveted to the movement of those large, tanned fingers against the crisp white of his uniform. One by one, the buttons gave way, baring a tantalizing glimpse of bronzed flesh. With a final tug at the Velcro fasteners holding the upright collar closed around his neck, he shrugged out of the jacket and reached for a hanger.

Abigail blinked at the expanse of rippling muscle that flexed with even the tiniest movement he made. With his back to her, she took advantage of the moment to drink in his magnificence. He'd taken off his hat as soon as they'd entered the room and now she could see how very blond his hair was. Had it always been that golden and that thick? she wondered. Cut in a blunt military style across the back, it emphasized the sculptured perfection of his neck and shoulders. Broader than she'd imagined, his upper torso tapered to a slim waist and narrow hips.

And the best set of buns she'd ever seen.

Her thoughts were flooded with memories of all the bold, sensual comments he'd made during their computer chats. In erotic terms, he'd managed to describe to her exactly where his hands and lips would be on her body when they were making love and how he would make her feel. He'd painted vivid pictures of their sweat-slickened bodies sliding together in passion...of how the bedclothes would get twisted around their bare legs...of how she would cry out from the pleasure he'd give her.

Abby couldn't tear her gaze away as he hung the jacket in the wardrobe, right next to a dark blue suit coat that was also heavily adorned with military braid and insignia. Lord, she'd always had a weakness for a man in uniform. And, as she was rapidly discovering, for a man *out* of uniform.

But when she saw his hands reach for his belt buckle and heard the rasp of a zipper going down, she panicked. It dawned on her that within seconds she would be sharing this incredibly small room with a naked or near-naked man.

Your husband, her conscience reminded her pointedly. "I can't—I mean we can't—you know—not now—not here—not like this—" Abigail stammered. Bert turned his head and gave her a questioning look, but didn't speak. "Look, I know I went into this with my eyes wide open. You and I both have reasons to see this thing through, at least for a while, so I can understand why it's prudent that we carry out the pretense when we're in public. But it would be dishonest of us if we were to act like husband and wife when we're in here, in the privacy of this room."

"Dishonest?" He took a step toward her. "Let's talk about dishonesty, Abby." There was a strange expression on his handsome features that only served to remind Abigail just how little she knew about this man with whom she'd just vowed to spend the rest of her life. Automatically she retreated until she backed against a solid, starkly painted wall.

He took another step before stopping. He was so close she could see the black spikes dividing the sky blue irises of his eyes. Cold, hard eyes. But there was something else she couldn't quite identify. If she didn't know better, she would have sworn there was a shadow of pain hiding behind the dispassionate stare. "What happened to the woman who likes making love with the soulful sounds of Kenny G drifting in the background?"

So here it was—*the* discussion they'd both been waiting for. She gulped, vividly remembering the night she'd sat in front of the computer, typing the words while a little imp sat on her shoulder, urging her on, compelling her to fabricate an alter ego for the dull, uninspiring Abigail Harris.

How could she tell him that the sexy lingerie, the champagne, the bubble baths and yes, even the love-making belonged to the risqué, and nonexistent, Angelina. Not the staid, predictable Abigail everyone knew and intellectually respected.

"So how many times have you done it, Abby?"

"Done what?" She tried to sound forceful, but realized she was failing miserably. A lump the size of Alaska had coagulated in her throat. Except for the night her car broke down and she had to walk home after midnight, she'd never experienced fear. But then again, she'd never been married to a perfect stranger who knew her better than any man ever had—better than even he knew.

He reached out. Her head connected with the wall behind her. Her pulse pounded, blood racing frantically. Anxiety paralyzed her, but she also had to admit feeling her first real frisson of excitement. Rationally she realized he would never hurt her. And yet...

With his right hand, he eased the errant, wind-blown strands of hair from her face. She felt the brush of his thumb across her ear, even heard the sound of his erratic breathing. "How many, Abby? One? Two? Three? A dozen?"

Why had she never noticed the subtle nuances of his voice before? "How many what?" she repeated, having a hard time grasping his words, her gaze so captivated by his unblinking stare. She might have felt ridiculous under normal circumstances, but she was quickly learning that nothing on the Ice was normal, that the line between reality and unreality was a confusing blur.

"Made love with Kenny G's sax in the background," he prompted when she didn't respond immediately to his inquiry.

Heated color rose to paint her cheeks. A fictitious lover on a nameless, sightless electronic bulletin board was one thing; talking about the nonexistent person with her *husband* not more than six inches away was another thing entirely.

He continued to rub the pad of his thumb around her ear, tantalizing her. "I bought a Kenny G tape before I left the U.S., Abby. Just for you. Just for us."

"Don't," she implored, wishing she could think, wishing he'd move away, wishing he wouldn't use her own words against her, wishing he wouldn't call her Abby in that soft, seductive way.

"Don't what?" He moved a fraction of an inch closer, so close their breaths mingled. He smelled of champagne, of wedding cake . . . of passion.

"Don't stand this close?" he prompted. "Don't remind you of the things you said to me? Or don't touch you like this? Or this?" He traced the outline of her lips. Though she tried to resist, her lips involuntarily parted. "You know, ever since we started corresponding, I've dreamed of this night." His voice was husky.

She tried to force herself to concentrate on what he was saying, rather than the way his fingertips felt against her suddenly ultrasensitive skin.

"I've dreamed of holding you in my arms, dreamed of stripping off your clothes, piece by piece. Dreamed of carrying you to the bed and..."

Her eyes drifted shut under the powerful onslaught. It was impossible to believe this was the same man she'd so casually dismissed in the lab, the flirtatious scientist who seemed more interested in the chemistry of mating Homo sapiens than the chemistry of molecules.

"I've dreamed of watching you climax, Abby, dreamed of hearing you call my name, asking for more."

"Bert..."

"Hmm? What part was it you didn't want to hear, Abby?" His fingers tightened on her jaw until her head was being gently, but very firmly held in place.

At the abrupt shift in his tone and the unexpected pressure of his hands, her eyes flew open. She saw he was angry—maybe even beyond angry. He was obviously upset about the situation, and Abigail wasn't sure which part of it bothered him the most—the fact that he'd married precipitously or that his mystery lover was Abby.

She'd been a fool to believe how wonderful things would be in Antarctica. For the first time, she'd let her heart rule her head and look where it had gotten her. Her fantasy had become a real-life disaster. And her Prince Charming had turned out to be a real-life toad.

"The part about me wanting to make love to you?" he went on, forcing her to continue looking into his wintry eyes. "Or the part about how you want to make love to me, *Angelina.*"

Bitterness welled up inside her. Bert was accusing her of being deceptive, conveniently ignoring his own part in the entire situation. "Look," she said angrily, surprising even herself with the defiance and vehemence in her tone, "I may not be totally innocent in all of this, but neither are you. You had plenty of opportunity back in Boulder to confess you were engaged in a steamy electronic love affair while you were asking me out."

"Confess?" Bert demanded. "What was I doing that you weren't doing just as often? You weren't exactly spilling your guts to me. You know that old saying about casting the first stone."

Anger at his accusations and his casual dismissal of his own guilt gnawed at her. She pushed away from the wall and pointed a finger at him. "If anyone has reason to feel deceived, it's me," she said.

"Honey, you wrote the book on deception."

"That's unfair and uncalled for."

"Really? I tried to get to know you better, but you never gave me the time of day. Imagine my surprise now, knowing you turned me down so you could hurry home and write hot messages to your fantasy lover saying you liked your kisses long and deep, the longer and deeper the better."

She remembered, only too well.

"I'll bet you'd have said things differently if you'd realized you were marrying me."

"You can count on that, Bert." The passion with which she made the statement shocked him. "For one, I wouldn't have married you."

He'd never seen this side of her before. At work she was calm, cool, even aloof. She'd been pretty enough. He'd known he wouldn't be in town long, but she'd seemed interesting and intelligent. He'd tried to date her because he thought it would have been a pleasant way to spend a few evenings. But it would have been more as a friendship—certainly not the type of relationship he wanted with the lover who'd haunted him day and night for the past few months.

But Abby as a spitfire was something completely new and, he had to admit, infinitely more interesting than the old Abigail. At work, she'd rarely stood up for anything, letting her work speak for itself. Now, with her large eyes snapping with sapphire sparks and her hands planted firmly on her slender hips, he felt a hint of the desire he'd felt for his computer lover.

"You're nothing but a two-timing Casanova," she continued, her nostrils flaring with barely contained fury.

For a second, he allowed himself to wonder what she'd look like with eyes darkened with passion instead of anger—the passion he'd dreamed of and longed for. But the passion she was bestowing on him at the moment wasn't the kind he wanted. And they were stuck together as man and wife, in the same room, and the same bed for the next four months.

"And furthermore, Captain Bert—"

"Call me Prescott."

She rolled her eyes. "You even went by an alias at work?"

"I had to." He hesitated, wondering just how much he should tell her about his assignment at BioGen. "Everything I told you on the computer is true. I *am* a captain in the United States Navy and also have my degree in biology with a minor in geology. But what I didn't tell you is that I work under cover whenever my specialties are needed. I can't go into the details, but BioGen has been receiving sizable grants from the government and their priorities were questionable. It was arranged that I work there on a special project so I could conduct an investigation. Bert Taylor was my operative name."

Through squinted eyes, she studied him, obviously trying to decide if he was telling her the truth or making up the whole story. He had to admit it sounded a little Hollywood even to him, but it was all true. So, being the excellent military strategist that he was, he decided to take the offense to throw her off. *And* get some answers of his own.

"I assume *you* weren't working under cover, *Angelina*." His eyebrow arched with just the right degree of sarcasm. "Or is under the covers where you work best?"

Her jaw dropped and her eyes widened at the implication. Then, with visible effort, she gathered her wits and faced him. "Okay, I'll admit that I probably gave you the wrong impression over the computer. I guess it was the anonymity or maybe I just felt very comfortable with Lobo, but I sort of let my fantasies take over."

"Why did you tell me your name was Angelina?"

Again, her discomfort was betrayed by the vivid color of her cheeks. Her voice lowered as she explained. "Because I didn't think Lobo would find Abigail very attractive."

The anger seeped out of him at the sincerity and the vulnerability in her tone. "And what's wrong with Abigail?" he asked, more because he didn't want to let the conversation drop than because he wanted to make her feel even worse.

With a sudden show of strength, she lifted her chin and looked directly into his eyes as she spoke of herself as if she were another person. "Nothing's wrong with Abigail. It's just that she's not beautiful and popular like her older sister Allison or vivacious and outgoing like her younger sister April or dedicated to keeping a spotless house and cooking a perfect meal like her mother was. Abigail was the *smart* one, the one who always turned in her homework and never missed a day of school. She used to try to straighten the curls out of her hair and put lemon juice on it so it would be silky blond like her sisters'. But it was too late. She'd been classified a brain and it wasn't cool to be that smart. She never went on a date in high school and only went on a couple in college with boys who were as brainy—and nerdy—as she was.''

The volume of her voice dropped again even though she didn't lower her gaze. "Then one day she met a wonderful, exciting man behind the protective curtain of a computer screen. He wouldn't be able to see how plain she was or know that she was totally inexperienced in the art of love. Instead she could flirt and pretend to be everything she'd ever wanted to be. And the name Angelina had just the right sound— exotic, sensual, beautiful.'' She shrugged. "I guess I was hoping that that man could fall in love with the woman inside and not judge her on anything else."

For a moment, Prescott softened, then the memory of how she'd rejected him so coolly back home resurfaced. The woman who had repeatedly turned him down hadn't been suffering from a lack of self-confidence, but from an overabundance of bitchiness. "That's a very touching story, Abby. But it doesn't wash," he said bluntly. "I've been on the receiving end of your frigidity, and I think you bring a lot of your problems with men on yourself. That is, if you really *do* have problems with men and aren't just making up another lie for me like you did on the computer. Or was the person on the computer the *real* one? She didn't sound like a bashful wallflower to me. You were a very convincing woman of experience, *Angelina.*"

Her expression changed like lightning from passivity to hostility. "Well, we both have our little fantasies, don't we? And we both have our little disappointments. But I just want to say that no matter what's true and what's not, you're just as much at fault as I am," she accused, not making any attempt to step away or break eye contact with him. "And, Captain Whoever-the-hell-you-are, I resent your implication that you're innocent while I'm a lying Delilah, scheming to trap you into marriage."

As much as he hated to admit it, she had a point. He wasn't completely innocent, yet for a reason he didn't understand and was unwilling to try to put a name to, Abigail's casual dismissal of him back home bothered him a great deal. At the time, it hadn't seemed so significant, but here, now that he knew what had been going on in her pretty head, it was very important.

But he had to admire her spunk. He had subordinates who weren't that brave. Angelina would have spoken up with equal vigor, but Abigail Harris in Boulder would have thought twice before being so confrontational. What the hell was it about the Ice that made things seem different than they really were?

"Look," he said, "accusations aren't going to solve anything at this point."

"No, they aren't," she agreed. "So where do we go from here?"

"A truce?"

"A truce? When you're convinced I'm nothing but—"

"Look, Abby, it doesn't matter what my opinion is of you. You don't have a much higher one of me right now. But we're both stuck here, and we're married."

"I just never imagined the for-better-or-worse part could be this bad." She sighed, the sound long and agonized, as if emerging from deep down inside.

"Honey, unless we call a truce, *this* is as good as it's going to get."

All the color drained from her face. Except for the blusher on her cheeks, she was completely pale, nearly as white as the wedding gown she wore. For a moment, compassion claimed him. "I can't live like this," she said softly.

"Then we're both going to have to live with a truce." Why had he never noticed how lovely she was? Her hair fell over the white velvet gown in a dark, silky cloud. And her eyes . . . why had he never seen the wide range of emotions that flowed across their depths?

"I suppose we both have to sleep here?"

He nodded, albeit reluctantly. He didn't relish sharing a bed with an ice maiden any more than she wanted to sleep with him. "Unless you'd rather sleep with penguins."

She wrinkled her nose.

"If either one of us goes looking for another roommate, particularly tonight, we're both going to be the subject of all sorts of gossip and innuendo.'' While he didn't mind what was said about him, Prescott realized he didn't want Abby talked about in uncomplimentary terms. "I'm afraid we're stuck, Abby."

She glowered at him.

"Bathroom's through that door. It's not very big, but it works. There's a shelf in the medicine cabinet for your personal items."

"Thanks."

"It's a truce, then?" he asked.

"For now," she answered softly. "Since we don't appear to have any other options."

"No. We don't." He stepped backward, trying to put a little emotional and physical distance between them.

Abby hesitated for a moment, then moved past him, closing the door with a firm click. Seconds later, he heard the sound of running water.

Prescott had never felt more uncomfortable than he did right now. Not only did he have a reluctant bride, but he was a more than reluctant groom. And there wasn't a whole hell of a lot he could do about either. Flights off the Ice were rare, nonexistent at some times of the year. Assuming the weather was good and mail or supplies were to be delivered, the next flight wouldn't arrive for two weeks.

He dropped onto the bed and tucked his hands behind his head. He stared at the ceiling while his mind painted a vivid—if not totally accurate—picture of what Abby was doing behind the closed door. The images were nothing new, however. Over the past few months while they'd been corresponding, he'd spent many a night imagining her relaxing in a bubble bath, cuddling under a billowy comforter, sliding silken hosiery up over shapely legs, and acting in all the other sexy scenarios they'd concocted. And oddly enough, after she'd given him a hint of what she looked like, it had been Abby's face in his fantasies all along. But they had never ended like this, with tensions, regrets and recriminations.

Abby emerged a half hour later, clutching her wedding gown against her chest. The snowy velvet cascaded over her arms and trailed along the floor around her bare feet. "You can hang that in the wardrobe," he commented.

Without a word, she turned to the small door and reached inside for the garment bag she'd brought. With her back to him, he couldn't help noticing that her oversize T-shirt left miles of skin open for view, but it definitely wasn't something he would have pictured on his bride for the first night of a honeymoon.

After all the contradictions in character he'd encountered with Abby, she could have been wearing anything from a lacy teddy to a high-necked, ankle-length flannel gown. He never would have guessed a T-shirt. Somehow he suspected that it hadn't been the garment she planned on wearing on her wedding night, but a last-minute substitution.

As Abby stood on her tiptoes to hang the garment bag back on the pole, the T-shirt rode indecently high on her thighs, stopping barely below her buttocks. Prescott sat up, taking in the sight of her, and swallowed a gulp. This was going to be a whole lot more difficult than he'd anticipated. There she was, in the middle of his room—their room—wearing nothing but a T-shirt and pink cotton panties. The way the material clung to the fullness of her breasts left no doubt she didn't sleep in a bra.

His stomach contorted, the intimacy of the situation gnawing at him. How the hell was he supposed to keep his hands off this very desirable woman—especially since she was legally his wife?

The look she gave him provided answer enough. He could keep his hands off because she didn't want him to touch her.

"I'm through in the bathroom," she said pointedly.

Taking the hint, he got up, moving with studied casualness. As he passed close to her he caught a whiff of perfume. Had she freshened it for him? Somehow he doubted it. But there was something about the way she looked, face devoid of makeup and freshly scrubbed, and something about the way her scent seemed to fill the room with her sweet, feminine essence that roused his masculinity to immediate attention. His steps quickened, and he slammed the bathroom door with more force than necessary.

He wasted no time as he immediately stripped and took a shower—a cold shower. Yet even as the icy drops of water streamed down his spine, he imagined her fingertips caressing the same path. Realizing the shower didn't provide even the slightest respite and knowing how precious water was on the Ice, he turned off the faucet.

After stepping out of the shower, he ran a towel roughly over his body and rubbed most of the moisture out of his hair, then opened the medicine cabinet. Even though he'd expected it, actually seeing her personal items on the shelves next to his was a little odd. Never in his adult life had there been a pink razor resting against his metal one in the Old Spice mug his father had given him.

For better or worse, the woman on the other side of the door was a permanent part of his life, at least temporarily. Under other circumstances, Prescott would have laughed at the humor of that contradiction. But contradiction seemed to be the theme of his and Abby's marriage. They were husband and wife only in public, not in private.

He shaved, though he realized he had little enough reason to. On a normal honeymoon night, he'd have shaved, being aware of how his evening shadow might feel on his wife's sensitive skin. But this wasn't a normal honeymoon, as he'd told himself often enough—and he had no doubt he wouldn't even hold Abby tonight, let alone make sweet love with her.

He swore as he nicked himself with the razor. Once again he was guilty of fantasizing instead of facing reality. After washing off the remaining cream, he slapped on some after-shave, wincing when it stung raw flesh.

Leaving the bathroom, he saw Abby in bed, snuggled under the blankets. She'd turned off all the lights so only the glow spilling out of the bathroom illuminated the area. "Abby?" he asked, walking across the floor.

She didn't answer. She lay on her side, her back toward the half of the bed she'd obviously assigned him. Her breathing wasn't even and rhythmic, so he knew she wasn't asleep. Obviously she was avoiding having to deal with him anymore tonight. Prescott turned off the bathroom light, returned to the bed, and climbed beneath the blanket, noting the way she stiffened slightly. For long minutes, he lay on his back, staring into the darkness, contemplating what to say, what to do to ease the tension. But nothing came to mind—nothing that wouldn't complicate things even more.

He let out a deep sigh. His honeymoon night was more of a disaster than he would ever have believed possible. Briefly he wondered how she would react if he took her in his arms and drew her close. Knowing Abby—or more precisely, not knowing Abby—he had no idea how she would respond.

Finally, Prescott turned his back to her, struggling again to ignore his body's natural reaction to sharing a bed with a desirable woman. After several hours of tossing and turning, he was forced to admit to himself that today had been the most unusual day of his life.

And he had a hell of a lot more of them ahead.

Chapter Four

It was still dark when Abigail opened her eyes. Trying to focus on the shadowy objects around her, she tried to reconstruct the jumble of memories from the last few days. Slowly it all came back to her as her sleepy brain began to wake up and function properly. If she remembered everything correctly, she was, at this very moment, at a scientific and military station in Antarctica, sharing a bed with her new husband.

Husband. Would she ever think or speak that word without that echo of disbelief? So far, marriage wasn't at all like she'd dreamed it would be.

Husband. Nervously, she tried to look backward, over her shoulder to see if he was still lying next to her. She had been very aware of exactly when he'd gotten into bed last night. She had been very careful not to move for fear there would be some sort of physical contact. And as much as her body wanted to be sexually fulfilled by this man with whom she'd thought she was in love, she'd been at a complete loss to know how to deal with such intimacy with Bert.

Prescott, she amended. Actually it was easier to think of him as Prescott because here on the Ice he wasn't anything at all like the Bert back in Boulder. She had felt his restlessness every time he turned over. Her intention had been to lie awake until he went to sleep to make sure their bodies didn't touch. But her own body had betrayed her. Severe jet lag had overcome her and pulled her into a sleep so deep she hadn't moved from the position she'd been in when she'd first lain down.

There was no motion or noise to indicate his presence, so she dared roll over just enough so she could see the other side of the bed. It was empty.

She didn't know whether to be relieved or annoyed. Did he care so little that he wouldn't even attempt to romance her or even keep up the pretense to the other residents of the station that they were blissfully married? Or did he care so much that he hadn't been able to sleep at all?

Abigail realized she was smiling at that thought and hugging her pillow with a lot more enthusiasm than was absolutely necessary. But a little voice inside her was telling her she should pack her bags and get out of here. She didn't need to spend another minute with a man who wouldn't know the truth if it slapped him in the face. His refusal to believe her had hurt. She'd opened up to him, and he'd rejected her flatly.

Before Abigail reached a decision, there was a light knock at the door. Then the knob turned and the door opened. "Are you awake yet, Sleeping Beauty?" The light from the hallway silhouetted his well-built body for a few seconds before he kicked the door shut behind him. "Mind if I turn on the light?"

Abigail automatically combed through the tangles of her hair with her fingers as she answered, "No, go ahead."

He flipped the switch and she blinked at the brightness. "I brought you some breakfast," he continued in a voice that was as neutral as it was cheerful.

For a moment, Abby was touched. But then she considered that he was probably just playing a role for the benefit of the rest of the people stationed at McMurdo. A man of his rank would have to be careful with appearances. "What time is it?" she asked, squinting at the clock radio on his side of the bed.

"Almost eleven." Prescott set the tray on the nightstand next to the clock, then sat on the edge of the bed. "You were sleeping so soundly, I didn't want to wake you earlier. I remember how long it took me to catch up on my sleep after coming here a week ago."

She sat up, being careful that her T-shirt was covering all the strategic feminine areas. The shirt had been a last-minute decision because she hadn't been able to put on the sexy nightie Allison had given her for her wedding night or the red teddy from Sandy. "I can't believe I slept so late. I never do that."

"You've flown through almost half a dozen time zones. Your body has no idea what time it is."

The fragrance of the food drifted to her nostrils, and her stomach growled, reminding her it had been a long time since she'd had a real meal. Even though there had been some sandwiches and chips to go with the wedding cake last night, she'd been so nervous she hadn't eaten a bite. "Thanks," she said, lifting her gaze to his. For a brief moment, she thought she saw a hint of genuine concern in his expression, but he turned away.

While she ate the scrambled eggs, crisp bacon and sipped at the hot, steaming coffee that, she assumed, was a necessity for survival here, she watched him, waiting for some sort of cue as to what was going to happen next. He didn't keep her in suspense for long.

"Since everyone expects us to be happy honeymooners, we aren't expected to jump back into the schedule of things until Monday. But I thought you might like a tour of the facilities today."

"Don't most people have the day off since it's Saturday?" Abigail asked as she finished the last bite of toast. Either she had been really hungry or the food was surprisingly good.

"They work a six-day week here and just have Sundays off," he explained. "But that's not as torturous as it seems. There's not much to do around here, so no one really minds having just one day off.

In fact, they tell me that on Christmas and other holidays when they have two days off in a row, everyone gets bored."

In a way, Abigail could understand that since she'd more or less been a workaholic for years. She could see how people involved in projects they truly enjoyed, especially for such a short, intense period of time, would prefer to keep focused on their work. "Can we go to the lab?" she asked. "I'd love to see what sorts of studies are under way."

"Except for a couple of secret projects, you'll have total access to any of the labs. I'm sure they'd love your input since you're so interested in the ozone layer. I'm sure you've heard that we're working with the Japanese on their latest ozone sensor."

Abigail sat up straighter, her interest piqued. "You mean the ILAS?"

"Yes, it's going to be mounted on a satellite and launched soon."

She threw back the covers and swung her legs out of bed, totally forgetting about modesty in her eagerness. "That's the most sophisticated system ever created to measure concentration, temperature and pressure in the ozone layer. I want to see whatever paperwork they've got on that."

"There're four Japanese scientists at the South Pole right now. They should be traveling back through McMurdo on their way home in about a week, so you'll have a chance to talk with them then."

Abigail opened her suitcase and frowned at the piles of clothes inside. "I guess I'd better unpack first. It won't take long."

"I'll help unload your CDC bags if you want me to," Prescott offered.

She pulled out a sweatshirt and gave him a tentative smile. "Thanks, I'd appreciate that. I have no idea what most of that stuff is for."

He picked up one of the two orange bags and put it on the bed. "You'll be very glad for it whenever you go outdoors. Even though it's relatively warm this time of year, the temperatures rarely rise above freezing."

"I doubt that I'll be outdoors very much except to go from building to building."

Prescott took a bright red parka out of the bag, shook it out and hung it on one of the coat hooks by the door. "I thought you and I might go on a day trip to the Dry Valleys when we have time. It's only about a hundred and twenty miles from here, and some of the more surprising fossils have been found in that area."

"Oh, I'd love that." Abigail's smile grew wider and more relaxed. She could handle conversations about science and the Gondwanaland supercontinent theory. It was just when the topics got personal or intimate that she began to feel uncomfortable. Flirting, even on the most harmless level, had never been one of her accomplishments.

Prescott paused, a pair of thick gloves in his hand, and looked across the small room to where she was standing. For just a moment, their gazes locked and they shared a smile—their first real smile.

"Will jeans be okay?" she asked, her voice strangely breathless. How had she never noticed that very attractive, masculine dimple in his left cheek? "For the tour, I mean."

"Sure. That's what most people wear around here, except for the military, of course. But even we dress as casually as possible."

Abigail added a pair of jeans to the pile of clothing in her arms and went to the bathroom to change. When she looked into the mirror, she groaned. With her hair tousled and not a drop of makeup on her face, she looked like the unsophisticated, ordinary-looking nerd that she was. All she needed was a plastic pocket protector and a pair of thick, tortoiseshell glasses to complete the picture. Lord, no wonder Prescott was turned off at the prospect of being married to her.

Abigail brushed her hair and was going to pull it into the familiar knot at the crown that kept the long, curly strands neatly in control, when a voice whispered in her ear, *Leave it down. Let yourself go for once in your life.*

Her fingers relaxed and the hair trickled out of her hand until it fell in a soft black cloud around her shoulders. With a touch of blusher on her cheeks and a soft rose lipstick on her lips, she pulled the black sweatshirt displaying the *Phantom of the Opera* logo over her head, then slid her legs into the black jeans. With a last, unreassuring glance in the mirror and a fervent wish that she was prettier and sexier, or at least not so plain, she opened the door and returned to the bedroom.

Prescott pulled out a pair of white boots from the second canvas bag, zipped it shut, then stored both of them under the bed next to his own. "I put your thermal underwear and insulated pants in the bottom drawer of your chest. You shouldn't need them today since we won't be outdoors for any length of time. Your gloves are in the pocket of your parka and here are your boots."

He pulled the sheets up and straightened the blanket and bedspread, but as he looked up, his hands stilled on the pillow. Although she was walking away from him, she was very aware that his gaze was following her. His attention excited her, yet made her nervous, and she hoped he wouldn't notice the way her fingers fumbled as she finished unpacking her suitcase, snapped it shut and slid it under the bed. When she turned around, she noticed his gaze was still focused on her.

"I never realized you had such beautiful hair, Abby," he commented at last, just when she thought she couldn't stand another second of silence. "Actually, I never realized you had hair... well, I knew you had *hair,* but I'd never really noticed it before."

She would have lifted her hand to smooth the thick, dark strands back from her face, but she stopped, aware that she was dangerously close to primping. And Abigail Harris *never* primped.

"Thanks," she murmured, wondering how many more times he was going to surprise her today. Or how many times she was going to surprise herself. Prescott lowered his gaze back to the bed and finished making it while Abby put on a pair of thick socks. "Should I wear the boots?"

"Yes, we'll be doing a lot of walking from building to building. I think it'll be better if we hit them all lightly today, then you can go back and explore them on your own."

"I guess you stay pretty busy with your troops or whatever you call them."

"I don't have *troops*. I'm the naval commander and my men are called seamen," he explained. "It *can* get pretty hectic, coordinating everyone and their assignments. But I'm enjoying it."

He held her parka for her while she slipped it on, then put on his own military green one. "Ready?" he asked as he held the door open for her.

She nodded, and as she walked past him, their parkas sliding together noisily, she realized she was indeed ready, eager, in fact, to get a good look at the place that would be her home for the next few months.

"The living and working area of McMurdo is only about a half mile square," Prescott began as they walked out of the dormitory and into the blindingly bright sunshine. After being in the artificial light of the bedroom, the brightness outside was startling. Abigail tried to shield her eyes, but the glare off the ice and snow was unbearable. "I put a pair of sunglasses in the right pocket of your parka," Prescott told her as he slid on a pair of mirrored aviator glasses.

She gratefully fished them out and put them on. "That's better," she sighed in relief. "I should have thought about that since I live in Colorado."

"Well, the sun's even worse here. I understand that later in the summer, some of the ice melts enough so we'll be able to see the ground." Abigail looked around at the endless stretch of snowy mountains. It was difficult to believe there was actually dirt under all that ice. "They say it's amazing because once the ice melts, lichen appear in green clumps all over the place, usually growing on the rocks. They go into a sort of freeze-dried condition during the winter, then come back to life in the summer."

Abigail was just beginning to feel the chill of the air against her bare cheeks when they arrived at the galley.

"You've already seen the mess hall, but I wanted to show you the store, the laundry room and the library that are all in this building." He showed her around, explaining procedure and protocol and introduced her to dozens of people. They even bumped into Sandy who was coming out of the store with a canvas bag of groceries.

"I see the two of you survived the night," Sandy said with a provocative wink. "I didn't expect to see you until Monday morning."

"I wanted to give Abby the official FNG tour," Prescott explained.

"FNG?" Abigail asked, confused at yet another term she didn't understand.

"The polite definition is Fairly New Guy. The gentleman in me won't allow me to tell you what the military definition is."

"Never mind. I think I can figure that one out for myself," Abigail said.

"Has he told you about Penny yet?" Sandy asked.

"Can't a man have any secrets?" Prescott rolled his eyes at Sandy, then slipped his arm around Abby's waist. "If you're trying to cause trouble between me and the little woman, you can forget it. Abby's a very understanding person, aren't you, *dear?*"

"Penny?" Abby echoed, feeling a strange sinking in the pit of her stomach. He had another woman? No wonder he wasn't welcoming his new bride with open arms.

"I'll confess all later," Prescott told her. "Let's get on with the tour."

Abigail had no option but to follow, even though the mysterious Penny still dogged her thoughts. But she was glad he dropped his arm from her waist and led the way into the library. Shelves of books and videotapes lined the walls, and there were piles of magazines on the tables.

"What sort of television programs do you get here?" she asked when she noticed the large-screen TV in the corner.

"Nothing current. Most of the programs are reruns from last year or earlier. And I'm sure you'll hate the news because it's from the Armed Forces Network and is disproportionately heavy on sports. But it's funny because after a week or two here, current events just don't seem that important. It's like we're on a different planet and whatever's happening in the rest of the world doesn't affect us one way or the other."

"I'll bet it's quite a shock to reenter the mainstream again," Abigail commented. She was trying very hard not to think about what she would be going back to. Would things work out between her and Prescott? Or would she be returning to her old job with her tail between her legs? Not to mention that she'd let her apartment go and had stored her furniture. And she didn't even want to think about what her sisters would have to say about "poor Abigail."

"I've heard it's strange, but not difficult to go home if you've spent only the summer here. But the winter-overs have a tough time readjusting. It's the silence and the lack of sunshine that gets people down the most." He pointed to a TV monitor mounted on the wall. "These are positioned throughout the station. Any special events are posted there, along with the day's menus. There's a disclaimer that they're always subject to change, which, I understand, happens quite a lot."

Abigail read the words as they scrolled down the screen. "What's pork adobo?"

"Oh, God, no! Please tell me we're not having pork adobo tonight." Prescott groaned. At her questioning look, he added, "It's a mystery-meat meal, and although I've been here only two weeks, we've had it a half dozen times. They just throw the word 'pork' in there to tease us. The meat is always questionable. I've learned to plan on eating out on those nights."

"There are restaurants here?"

"No, but one of the clubs has a grill night a couple times a week." He glanced at the date on his wristwatch. "Unfortunately tonight's not one of them." He gave her a conspiratorial smile. "But I just happen to have a stash of food I brought with me. I had a friend tell me to ship a supply of quickie foods to myself from the U.S. before I left. And lucky for you, I'll share."

His grin was so wide and infectious that Abigail couldn't keep from giving him a smile in return. Why hadn't she ever noticed this charming, irresistible side of his personality before?

They walked back through the galley and put on their coats in the entry area. "We'll head toward the science building, but we'll pass a couple other places along the way, including McMurdo General."

"Why do I suspect that that's not really a hospital?" she commented, rapidly growing aware that very few things were "normal" on the Ice.

"Actually they call it an infirmary, but it's more of a dispensary. There's just one doctor and he has a few corpsmen drop in to help out. So, unless you're *really* sick, you probably should avoid that place except for social visits."

Prescott pushed open the door and once again the brilliance of the sunshine caught Abigail by surprise. "Do you ever get used to twenty-four hours of daylight—especially such *bright* daylight?"

"I haven't yet, but I imagine it's a lot easier to get used to continuous day than continuous night."

Abigail fumbled for her sunglasses as she took a step outside. But, blinded by the glare, she couldn't see the obstacle in front of her until she tripped over it. There was a loud, shrill chirp, followed by a sharp pain on her ankle. She stumbled, caught between taking a step forward and automatically trying to retreat. If it hadn't been for Prescott's quick reflexes, she would have fallen.

After she recovered her balance and pushed her sunglasses firmly into place, she looked down and saw the source of her problem. "It's a penguin!" She leaned over to rub the sore spot. "I've been attacked by a wild penguin."

"Not exactly wild," Prescott corrected. "Abby, meet Penny. You'll have to watch out for her. She's always underfoot."

"*That's* Penny?" Abigail hoped she didn't sound as relieved as she felt.

"She thinks I'm her mother."

Abigail's gaze swept up and down his tall, very well-developed frame. "I've never seen a six-foot penguin."

"Six foot one, but who's counting."

She shook her head and groaned. "Okay, I stand corrected. I've never seen a six-foot-one-inch penguin."

"It's not the appearance but the timing, apparently. You see, I was working in the supply warehouse the first couple of days I got here so I could familiarize myself with the inventory the navy is responsible for maintaining." He scratched Penny's sleek black head. She responded by rubbing her bill against his leg in an undeniably affectionate gesture.

"I was sitting on the loading dock early one morning, eating a doughnut and trying to wake up. It's very disorienting when it looks like high noon no matter what time of the day you get out of bed. Anyway, I was sitting there and a whole flock of penguins ambles over and starts trying to jump up onto the dock. It's about four feet off the ground, so they weren't being too successful. I tried shooing them away, but they were determined to get up there. Well, I found out later that the supply warehouse had been built on their old nesting grounds, and even though that was more than fifty years ago, old instincts die hard, so a few birds come back every year."

Penny was making happy little chirping sounds that were so sweet that Abigail was tempted to reach down and pet the small bird. But every time Abby made any sort of movement, the penguin's bright, round, glassy-looking eyes took on a warning glow that clearly told Abigail that the only human Penny was interested in was Prescott. "She looks like she'd like to go for my throat," Abigail commented.

"She's a little possessive. I'm trying to break her of that. I've been thinking that maybe I should try to find her a handsome, unattached boy penguin."

"They'd both be dressed for the wedding." Abigail couldn't resist smiling at the small creature's attachment to its unlikely friend. "So, go on with your story."

"Okay, I was sitting there—"

"I got that part."

He gave her a quelling look, but the twinkle in his light blue eyes took away any hint of anger. "I heard a squeaking sound and I looked down and saw that the other penguins were hopping onto poor little Penny, using her for a step stool. I chased them away. Penny just lay there for a few seconds, and I thought she wasn't going to make it. But she gave a little peep, then dragged herself to her feet, waddled over to me and leaned against my leg." His smile was a little sheepish. "Except when she's sleeping or out swimming, she follows me everywhere."

Abigail laughed, as much for Prescott's obvious embarrassment as for Penny's equally obvious infatuation. "I think it's more than a father/daughter thing. She's in love with you."

"Well, she'll just have to get over me," Prescott bantered back. His tone was light, but his eyes were watching Abby sharply as he added, "I'm a married man now."

Abby had faced stiffer competition than a confused penguin...and lost. But she'd never cared more about the outcome. However, she dared not let him know how she really felt. Either he wouldn't believe her or it wouldn't matter to him one way or the other. Abby's only hope was that she could hold on long enough to see if there was even the tiniest spark of Lobo left inside him on which they could build a loving relationship. And to keep her pride and her sanity while she waited, she couldn't let him know how much it mattered to her.

"Well, Penny will have you all alone again soon enough," Abby replied lightly. "Obviously, sir, you've been at sea too long if you go for females with beady eyes and fishy breath."

Chapter Five

By the time they'd finished touring the three-story lab building, Abigail was yawning. Since the sun appeared to be moving in a slow circle around the sky instead of rising and setting, it was impossible to tell what time of day it was. All she knew was that she was still exhausted.

Prescott had proven to be surprisingly good company. It was so odd that she hadn't been interested in carrying on a five-minute conversation back in Colorado unless they were talking about a BioGen project, yet here in this farthest outpost of civilization they had been chattering all afternoon. He'd told her about his military career and how he'd been on active duty for ten years and in ROTC for two years at college. She'd tried not to show her envy as he described all the places he'd traveled to around the world, as well as his long-term assignments in Europe and a brief stint in Russia. For a woman who'd grown up at the foot of the Rocky Mountains of Colorado, never having traveled more than a hundred miles in any direction until a few days ago, his stories were fascinating.

In the back of her mind was the nagging thought that he must have had at least one woman in each of those dozens of ports. The envy took on a jealous tinge that Abigail could neither understand nor explain. On the one hand, she had no idea what would become of her marriage. But on the other hand, she wasn't too crazy about the idea that she was just one of many.

And there was the even more unnerving prospect that she didn't measure up. With her complete lack of experience, how would she ever be able to make him happy? In spite of all the lectures her mother had given her, Abigail was becoming a little embarrassed about being the last thirty-year-old virgin in the Western Hemisphere. It had gotten past the point of being a quaintly sweet characteristic. Just like applying for work, it took experience to get a job, but it took having a job to get the experience.

Well, it wasn't a problem she would have to deal with immediately. And yet...

Abigail sneaked a surreptitious glance at her husband as they walked back toward their room. The sunlight danced playfully on the blond strands of his hair, sparkling in the interwoven threads of gold-and-silver silk. His piercing blue eyes were hidden behind his sunglasses, and instead of staring at her own reflection in their mirrored lenses, her gaze drifted down to his lips. As they moved, forming words, stretching into a wide smile or barely curving in a teasing grin, she couldn't keep from thinking how soft and sexy they appeared.

It wasn't the first time she'd imagined how they would feel beneath her own. Although she was getting to know him better, even to the point of having a whole new set of fantasies, more than likely she would never find out exactly how soft his lips were. He obviously wasn't having the same sort of thoughts. Without sparks, there could be no flame. The best she could hope for with Prescott would be friendship.

A part of her knew that friends are the most wonderful treasures a person can have. But another part recognized that while friends are great, being truly, deeply, madly in love would be the best thing in the world. Not for the first time in recent days, Abigail had to agree with her wilder, more impractical side.

"So, what would you like to do for dinner tonight?"

Abigail's thoughts scattered as Prescott's question penetrated her consciousness. "What sort of choices do we have?" she asked.

"Well," Prescott drawled, his expression deadpan, "we can dine on the ever-unpopular pork adobo deluxe in the mess hall, nibble on pretzels and popcorn at one of the bars or heat up something in our room."

"Define 'heat up something in our room.'"

"Abby, you have a very suspicious mind." His intriguing lips curled into an appealing, but naughty grin. "Not only suspicious, but dirty. I like that in a woman." Abigail glared at him with as much censure as she could muster. His voice was drippingly innocent. "I was talking about the hot plate in our room and that stash of goodies from home. What did you think I meant?"

At the moment, safety in numbers sounded like a good idea. She was afraid that if they spent the long hours of the evening alone in their room the conversation would falter, or worse, decline into arguing. It had flowed so easily today that she didn't want to press her luck. "I think dinner in the galley sounds like fun," she retorted. "I'd like to try the pork adobo. We can even give a prize to the person who identifies the ingredients first."

"I don't think I want to know," Prescott commented with a grimace.

There was quite a crowd in the mess hall when they arrived. Sandy explained it was because of the fresh vegetables that had been flown in on the same flight on which Abigail had arrived yesterday. Apparently, "freshies," as they were called, were a treat not to be missed.

They found an empty table on the officers' side of the room. Although there were no visible divisions in the room, the military was formally divided into an officers' and an enlisted side, but the civilians were free to choose either location. Sandy and Bill followed Prescott and Abigail through the cafeteria-style line, then sat across from them. A very nice divorcée named Diane whom Abby had met in the lab during her tour joined them with her boyfriend.

"What did you think of the facilities?" Bill asked Abby. "I don't get in there much, but I've heard the science lab is state of the art."

"It seems to be," she responded. "I'm looking forward to working there. They're doing some very interesting studies. Who knows what sort of impact their findings will have on our environment?"

"I'll show you where all the files on the ozone projects are kept," Diane offered. "I never really worried about it until I came down here last summer. Do you realize the opening is now 8.9 million square miles? About three times larger than the continental United States."

"Enough shop talk," Sandy interrupted. "It's Saturday night and you know what that means."

Abby waited, hoping Sandy would fill her in on the significance of the evening.

"Toga, toga, toga!" Bill responded enthusiastically.

Abigail sent Prescott a questioning look, and he responded with a chuckle. "No, we don't actually dress in togas and feed each other grapes," he explained. "Around here, Saturday night is party time, and that's just their way of saying it's time to boogie."

"Ah...boogie," Abigail echoed and nodded knowingly. "I understand boogie."

"Do you now?" Prescott asked, one sandy brow lifting in a teasing arch.

"I may not have a chance to go out much, but I *do* know how to dance." Abigail was quick to defend herself.

Prescott scooted his chair back noisily. "Then what are we waiting for? Are you guys up for the Acey-Deucy? Or should we stick with the old-timers at the Chiefs' Club?"

Sandy's brown eyes sparkled. "I feel like rockin' the night away. But then, Bill and I are old married folk." She winked at Abby. "We've been married almost a month, so we don't mind staying out all night. But I suppose you newlyweds will want to get home early."

"No!" Abigail and Prescott spoke simultaneously, then exchanged sheepish glances.

"I mean..." Prescott began, his gaze sliding away from Abby's. "I'm sure Abby wants to see how we live here and meet as many people as she can."

"Well, the Acey-Deucy isn't exactly where the beakers usually hang out," Bill commented as they left the galley after putting on their outdoor gear.

This time Prescott didn't even wait for Abigail to ask. "'Beakers' is the nickname for the scientists."

"It sounds sort of derogatory."

"It's not really," Sandy explained. "On one hand, the divisions between civilians, the military and the scientists are very marked. But on the other hand, it's just one big family. Take me, for example. I work with computers in the main office and would have had to share a dorm room with one of the other civilians. But because Bill's in the navy and we're married, I can stay with him in the officers' wing."

"I was curious about the sleeping arrangements for everyone else." Actually, Abigail was wondering if there was any place she could move to if the relationship between her and Prescott became too uncomfortable. It never hurt to find out more about her options.

The other five exchanged amused grins as if sharing an inside joke. Prescott spoke quickly. "If you mean how many people are assigned to a room, it's usually two. The civilian dorms are coed except for Jamesways. That's where the first-year men stay, and they're way on the other side of the base. We didn't go that far on our tour."

"But if you want to know where everyone spends the night," Diane remarked suggestively, "then that's another matter entirely."

"Is there a lot of, er, that going on here?" Abigail didn't know how to phrase her question more delicately.

"It does get pretty lonely, and everyone's a long way from home. Some people cope by working constantly, some by spending their time off in the bars and some by getting involved in relationships. Many of these don't go further than friendship, but quite a few get into what we call Ice marriages." Diane shrugged her shoulders. "These so-called marriages rarely work out. I don't know, there's something unique about this place. It's like we're on another planet, and there's nothing or no one beyond Mc-Murdo Sound. When they get back to the real world, it's different."

Abigail noticed Prescott's cool blue eyes focused on her and she wondered if he was thinking the same thing she was. The odds against them making a success of this impulsive marriage were increasing constantly. They didn't even have a strong physical attraction to hold them together. After all, they'd slept side by side in a double bed without Prescott making any attempt to touch her.

She sighed, hoping to expel some of the confusion and frustration she was feeling. Did she really want to have to fight off his advances? Or was she disappointed that she didn't have to? Loneliness was no stranger to her, but maybe the isolation of these surroundings magnified it. Or was the magic of the Ice getting to her already?

Loud music blared through the closed door, declaring more succinctly than any signs that they had arrived at the club. Before Abigail had a chance to question her decision to go dancing, Sandy and Diane swept her inside with Bill, Diane's boyfriend, Richard, and Prescott following behind.

The small building was packed with people standing four and five deep at the bar. The three women were immediately surrounded by men until one of them saw Prescott and said, "Hey, it's the captain's wife. Back off, fellas."

"She sure is purty, isn't she?" a young sailor with a rich South Carolina drawl said.

"I'm sure he wouldn't mind sharing her since there's so few women here," one of the other men added. "It would do wonders for our morale."

The Southern seaman stepped forward and saluted Prescott. "Requesting permission to dance with your lady, sir."

Prescott returned the salute. "It's up to her, John." He glanced at Abigail and their gazes locked.

Why was he so quick to let her go? Did he dread dancing with her so much? Well, she'd show him she wasn't a boring little wallflower.

"Ma'am, would you do me the honor?" the young man asked and held out his hand.

With a dazzling smile, Abigail placed her hand in his. "Thanks, I'd be delighted." With a toss of her dark hair, a very *un*-Abigail-like action, she let him lead her to the small dance floor.

A small band jammed in the corner, providing surprisingly good imitations of current rock and roll hits. There were so many people crammed into the small space that it really didn't matter whether or not Abigail was a good dancer. It quickly became apparent that the fancy moves didn't interest John so much as the companionship. Even though he had to shout to be heard, he told her about his family back home and how much he missed them. "Shoot, when I joined the navy, I expected to sunbathe on a beach in the Caribbean, not freeze my butt, er, behind off in Antarctica."

Abigail laughed along with him. "At least by the time you get back home it'll almost be summertime. Maybe you'll get stationed at Virginia Beach. That wouldn't be too far from your family."

"With my luck, they'll send me to Greenland next." He gave her a crooked grin. "Or Kansas. I don't know which would be worse."

One of the other sailors tapped John on the shoulder. "You've monopolized her long enough. It's my turn."

Before Abigail had time to protest, John stepped away, although he did it reluctantly. But he was soon replaced by another eager sailor, then another and another until she could no longer remember all their names. All she knew was that she had never before felt so pretty and desirable in her life. As the music pulsed through her and her dance partners crowded closer, waiting for their turn, she felt she knew what it would be like to actually be an Angelina.

Her logical side tried to remind her that since nine hundred of the twelve hundred people here were men, even the homeliest woman would be desirable.

But she refused to listen. The men who continued to vie for her attention stood in contrast to her husband. All evening Prescott had sat at the bar, not dancing with anyone, just watching her. At times she'd thought there might be a hint of longing in his expression. But then the next time she glanced his way, he would be deep in conversation or laughing along with someone else as if completely oblivious of her.

"Okay, so I *want* him to notice me," she admitted in a mental dialogue with herself. "He's a very attractive man and the more I get to know him, the more I like him. Besides, it shouldn't be that hard to rekindle those fires that were burning through the keyboard just a few days ago."

"Would you like to dance, ma'am?" a voice behind her asked, but she shook her head.

"I'm a little tired," she answered. "I think I'll sit this one out." It wasn't an excuse—she was feeling a little shaky. As she took a step toward the bar, her legs wobbled and she reached out to hold on to the back of a chair to steady herself. Although she'd stopped moving on the dance floor, it still seemed to be spinning around her. A chill chased its way through her body, followed immediately by a hot flash that left her skin feeling clammy.

"You've danced with every other guy in the place, so how about . . ." She looked up into Prescott's slate blue eyes, but his face was fuzzy and out of focus. "My God, Abby, you look like you're going to faint!" he exclaimed.

"Don't be ridiculous. I've never fainted in my—"

"IS SHE DOING ANY BETTER?" A female voice floated faintly on the heavy mists of her dream.

"Her fever's down and she's been trying to wake up, but she doesn't seem to be able to," a male voice answered, the worry evident in his tone. "I just hope she's going to be okay. If anything happens to her here, I'll never forgive myself."

"She's going to be fine," the woman stated with complete confidence. "You were lucky not to catch this bug when you first arrived. Almost everyone else does. It's something like a bad case of flu. It just has to run its course."

"I hope you're right." The man was obviously still doubtful.

Abigail felt cool fingers gently stroke her forehead, pushing her hair back from her face. The touch felt so good that she hoped it would never go away. One of the few things she could remember from her dream was how prickly and hot she'd felt.

"Look, she's smiling," the man said. "Do you think she can hear us?"

"Maybe she's trying to wake up. It's been three days."

"Abby, sweetie, how do you feel?" The male voice penetrated the mist with a forcefulness that compelled her to open her eyes.

It took more of an effort than she expected, but she finally managed to force her heavy eyelids upward. The bright lights made her squint at the two shadowy figures above her. Slowly the indistinct edges of the forms sharpened until she could recognize Sandy's friendly face. Abigail shifted her head slightly until Prescott's handsome features also came into focus. "Hi," she said, her voice weak, but clear. "What's going on?"

The hand on her forehead lifted and Prescott leaned back. "She's back." His voice trembled with relief.

"Where've I been?" Abigail asked. Moving her head slowly because she had a pounding headache, she looked around the stark white room. "For that matter, where am I now?"

"You're in the infirmary," Sandy answered, then lowered her voice to add, "Now that you're awake, we'll get you out of here as quickly as possible."

Abigail shifted uncomfortably on the narrow cot. Now that the mist was clearing, she was becoming painfully aware of her surroundings. She tried to draw in a deep breath, but her lungs objected and sent her into a coughing spasm. Prescott handed her a glass of water and hovered next to her while she managed to take a few sips. "What happened?" she finally managed to croak. "Last thing I remember...we went dancing...the room was hot and crowded...the music was very loud."

"You were struck by what we unaffectionately call the McMurdo Crud," Sandy explained as she went to a bureau, opened a drawer and took out Abigail's clothes.

"But I've been here only a little more than twenty-four hours. It's medically impossible to catch anything that quickly."

"Actually you've been here for four days because you lost a few while you were down with the crud." Sandy handed Abigail a hairbrush and a mirror. "And even though it defies science, it hits a lot of FNGs quick and hard. I've heard it's because of all that freezing, extremely dry air you're sucking into your lungs. It takes some bodies by surprise, and you were one of the unlucky ones. But the good news is, you got it out of the way and don't have to worry about it sneaking up on you later. We're still waiting for the captain to take his turn in here."

Abigail looked in the mirror and grimaced. Her complexion was deathly pale, almost as white as the scratchy sheets on the cot. Dark circles made her eyes look even larger than usual and her black hair was a torrent of tangles.

"Well, I've got to run. I'm on my lunch break and have to get back to the office." Sandy reached for her parka and pulled it on. "Bill and I'll stop by your room tonight and check on you." She turned to Prescott. "You're going to take her home now, aren't you?"

"As soon as she gets dressed," he confirmed.

"And I suppose you'll be more than capable of helping her do that," Sandy teased. She gave them both a jaunty wave and left.

Abigail looked up at Prescott. "What did she mean by that?"

"I...uh...somebody had to take care of you while you were sick, and I *am* your husband, so..."

Realization began to dawn on her and Abigail lifted the sheet to find she was now wearing only her over-size T-shirt and a pair of panties. She didn't remember exactly what she'd been wearing the night they'd gone dancing, but she was positive it hadn't been that.

Memories of weak-kneed trips to the bathroom while she'd had to lean heavily on someone's strong arm to get there and back pushed through the mists. She recalled someone bathing her feverish body with cold washcloths, and the murmur of gentle, soothing words, and the comfort of being held against a broad chest as she was carried to the infirmary.

"You?" she asked hesitantly. "You mean...the bathroom? The baths? Undressing me? Everything?"

He nodded after each question, then added an apologetic shrug.

"Did you come here often?"

"I stayed with you all the time," he answered. "The doctor is running himself ragged. There are a couple dozen other people down with the crud, and I wanted you to have full-time treatment." Again he shrugged. "I guess I feel responsible for bringing you here."

"Oh." For just a moment she had felt a surge of hope that he actually cared about her. But he'd made it clear that it was only his displaced sense of responsibility that caused his concern, not any sort of affection.

She sat up, her hands pressed against her pounding temples. When the room stopped spinning, she reached for her clothes and pulled them closer. "I realize you've already seen everything, but would you mind giving me a little privacy while I get dressed?"

His gaze automatically moved down her body, lingering where the T-shirt clung to the rigid points of her breasts. "Yeah, sure, I'll be right outside," he said, switching his attention back to her face. He turned toward the door, then stopped and looked over his shoulder at her. "You had me worried, Angelina." Before she could respond, he gave her a tired smile and left the room.

Angelina. It was the first time he'd called her that with affection since she'd arrived. And from those sensuous lips the name had sounded even sweeter and sexier than it had appeared on the computer screen.

Hmmm... Maybe, just maybe, he truly cared about her. Abigail felt a fresh wave of optimism as she replaced her T-shirt with the sweatshirt and jeans she must have been wearing on Saturday night.

Maybe, just maybe, this marriage would work out after all.

Chapter Six

"Mail call!"

A murmur of excitement ran through the mess hall, and the rattle of cutlery against plates ceased as if on command.

"Everyone lives for mail call," Sandy explained, pushing aside her partially eaten lasagna. "Anything to break the routine and give us some news from home." She wadded her napkin and tossed it onto the tray. "Coming?"

"I doubt there's anything for me," Abigail said. "I haven't been here long enough for my family to write to me."

"Oh, come on, anyway. I'm tired of looking at your mopey face."

"Mopey?"

"Mopey," Sandy said with ringing finality.

Abigail had to admit the diversion would be really welcome. Since she'd arrived and formed a truce, if not a friendship with her husband, she'd had little enough excitement in their relationship. During the two weeks she'd been at the station, she'd immersed herself in her work, and was very pleased with the results. Besides meeting with the Japanese scientists and discussing their experiments, she'd set up a small aquarium next to the large one already established so she could perform a study of the life-forms that were thriving under the ice shelf.

Since she was on her way back to the lab, anyway, she agreed to go along with Sandy. "Why not?"

Mail call reminded her of some of the old war movies she'd seen. People gathered outside the galley, anxiously waiting for their names to be called, alternately excited then disappointed as each letter or package was pulled from the postal sack. Other than by very limited and expensive telephone calls, this was their only contact with the outside world and all the friends and relatives they'd left behind.

Abigail caught sight of Prescott on the far side of the crowd. The always-brilliant sun shining on his hair gave it a healthy gleam. Even among the hundreds of men at the base, many in uniform, he stood out. He'd made it a habit to join her for lunch, but today he'd joined some of his officers for a business luncheon in one of the conference rooms outside his office.

She thought about trying to make her way over to him, but decided against it. Ever since she'd recovered from the crud, they'd been getting along better. He was everything she could ask for in a friend—attentive, sweet, patient and always able to make her laugh. She tried not to think about the reasons why he still hadn't made any attempt to make love to her... or even kiss her. Maybe he was trying to give her the time and space he thought she needed to adjust both to married life and the Ice. Or maybe—no, she refused to contemplate any other possibilities.

"Sandy Schultz."

Abigail shared a smile with her friend before being abandoned as Sandy ran forward, took her letter and wandered off to the side to read it. As the minutes passed and the crowd thinned, Abigail began to feel like an outsider. Her gaze kept returning to her husband, and she wished he would make the first move and come over to her.

Incredibly, he looked up, caught her stare and smiled. Abby's heart gave an odd lurch, and instead of looking away, she smiled back.

"Bert Taylor!" The man calling names peered around, confusion on his face.

"That's for me." Prescott quickly stepped forward and took the envelope. He glanced at the writing, then looked over at Abigail.

Realization dawned on her and she felt the chill of an Antarctic wind. She was one of the few people here who had ever known him as Bert. Without even seeing the handwriting, she knew he held the letter she had written to him—or rather to Bert—the day before she left, breaking their date. Her stomach twisted into a knot.

She knew how he felt about the way she'd snubbed him then. Worse yet, she'd been very blunt in her letter, telling him that she wasn't interested in him now or ever, and that she thought he was shallow and frivolous. But she'd closed it with an apology for having to cancel out on the lecture, even though she'd been careful to make sure he knew she hadn't considered it a date.

It wasn't possible. Not now that they'd managed to reach some sort of comfortable understanding and were beginning to build on it. And yet he held in his hands what he would interpret as further proof that she had judged him too quickly.

"One more package, sir."

Prescott took hold of a large box firmly secured with tape and tucked it under his arm. Then he saluted her with the envelope and walked toward his office.

A maelstrom of conflicting emotions whirled inside her. Obviously her husband thought her letter was filled with the sort of scientific discussion that had been the basis of their relationship before they met on the Ice.

But it wasn't. It was the "Dear Bert" letter she thought he'd received before she'd left. Abigail panicked. She had to get the letter from him before he had the opportunity to read it. Turning, she started after him. She was afraid she'd lose all the ground they'd gained if he beat her to it.

"Abigail Harris!" She paused, watching Prescott's tall form disappear around the corner of the galley. "Abigail Harris?" the young clerk repeated.

"That's me," she said, finally realizing he was calling her. Fingers as numb as her mind, she accepted a letter, mumbling what she hoped was coherent thanks. She didn't stop to look at the writing, but continued trying to catch Prescott.

He was in his office with the door open, his blond head bent over a report. Her letter lay atop the desk, unopened. Abigail knocked on the doorjamb. Without looking up, Prescott waved an invitation. Her heart pounding, she entered.

"Be right with you," he said.

She closed the door, resting her shoulders against the solid support of wood. She debated whether she should just snatch the letter and run. But he was obviously faster, and if she made such a big deal about it, he'd definitely want to read the contents. Her only hope was never to let him read the letter in the first place.

After what couldn't have been more than thirty seconds, but felt like an hour, he pushed aside his papers and gave her a warm, easy grin. "Abby, you should have said something. I wouldn't have kept you waiting."

She shrugged. "I know how busy you are."

"I can always make time for my wife."

Two weeks ago, he wouldn't have said that. But as slowly as summer deepened on the vast frozen continent, their relationship had begun to thaw. Now Abby felt as if she was balanced on a precipice, waiting for any little gust of wind to send her over the edge. The letter, sent to Bert in care of BioGen since she hadn't had his home address, would do it.

Prescott had made no attempt to hide how he felt about her actions. Apparently he'd been hurt that she'd never taken the time to get to know him better before she'd decided he wasn't suitable. And the letter was more damning evidence.

It certainly wouldn't help their marriage when he read that she thought he had nothing to offer her, and that they were very different personality types. She'd also said that it had been a mistake to accept his invitation and for him not to bother trying to contact her because she was leaving the country on a research trip.

Why hadn't she mentioned that she was in love with someone else? Even that might have tempered the blow. Instead, in retrospect, her letter seemed unnecessarily harsh and cold, which would only reinforce Prescott's earlier conclusions. And as she well knew, scientists dealt in facts, all of which did nothing to prove she wasn't a snob.

"What can I do for you?" he asked.

She hadn't thought much past getting in his office. "I was wondering what we're doing for dinner."

"Same thing as always. Why, did you have something else in mind?"

She was saved from a reply by a knock on the door. One of Prescott's subordinates entered with instructions for the captain to report to the communications center where there was a message from his commanding officer in the States. That meant he would be forced to leave his office—maybe providing her with the only chance she had to get rid of the letter that could otherwise destroy whatever future she might have with him.

"I'll be there in a few minutes," Prescott said. The other man saluted smartly, then pivoted and left. "About dinner?" Prescott prompted.

"I thought maybe we could stay in our room tonight." What on earth was she going to cook on their single burner? They'd almost exhausted their supply of canned chili and spaghetti. Maybe a new shipment had come in the box he'd received today.

"Sounds...promising." The lopsided grin she'd so rarely seen made her heart skip a beat. Maybe two. This was the Lobo she'd fallen in love with over the impersonal computer terminal. "You cooking?" he asked.

"If you don't mind being a guinea pig."

"I'll help you. I think I've even got a bottle of chardonnay stashed somewhere."

She smiled a tight, false smile. If she didn't get hold of the letter, there wouldn't be a dinner, pleasant or otherwise.

"Unfortunately, duty calls." He stood and smoothed the wrinkles out of his uniform slacks.

She stepped aside, hoping he'd pass, leaving her alone for the precious few seconds she needed to grab the destructive evidence. He didn't give her the chance. Instead he turned off the light, then placed his palm on the small of her back, guiding her from the office ahead of him.

"What's that?" He nodded his head at the letter she was holding.

She looked at her hand, having forgotten she'd received mail, too. "I have no idea who it's from."

"Maybe it's from another fantasy lover," he said as he gave her a flirtatious wink.

She flushed, remembering he'd been her fantasy lover—until reality had turned into something surreal. "More than likely it's from my father, although I can't imagine why he'd be writing to me. Ever since my mother died four years ago, he's kept to himself."

"I hope it's not bad news." Prescott gave her a sympathetic smile. "I'll see you this evening." He reached for the knob, pulled the door closed behind them and wiggled the knob to be sure it was locked.

"Yeah. Sure." For a few seconds, she watched his retreat.

He stopped and turned to face her. "And Abby?"

"Yes?"

"I'm looking forward to tonight."

"So am I," she lied.

Without another word, he turned once more. His highly polished black shoes echoed off the cold tiles, the precise tapping sounding like a military color guard marching on their way to a dawn execution.

And the execution was hers.

ABBY WAS ACTING differently. But, he mentally amended, giving up the pretense of trying to work, she was acting more like the Angelina he'd learned to love over a computer. Like the wife he'd always wanted but had nearly given up ever finding.

Prescott propped his feet on the desk, then leaned back in his chair. It'd been a hell of an adventure since she'd arrived on the Ice—actually since the fateful day he'd decided to respond to her comments on the electronic bulletin board.

And now he was married. Married to a woman he'd thought he knew, but really didn't have a clue about. But discovering the real Abby was turning into a lot of fun.

Things had started to warm up between them in the past few days. His own feelings had still been ambivalent until that evening when she'd fainted in his arms. Protesting the whole time that she wasn't going to, she'd gone deathly pale and would have collapsed onto the floor at his feet had he not caught her. She was tough and fragile at the same time—an intriguing combination.

And there was something about taking care of her while she'd been sick, sitting beside her day and night and worrying about her that had created a powerful bond. When she had regained her strength, he'd still caught himself hovering over her, almost smothering her with his care. He'd felt so responsible for her being there in the first place, that her illness had made him reevaluate their relationship. A lot of hurdles lay ahead of them, but he knew he didn't want to lose her. Things certainly weren't boring with her around.

And they promised to get even more interesting tonight. He still didn't completely trust her; maybe he never would. Yet he was game to try to make the marriage work, if possible. He realized they'd gotten off to a bad start. But the attraction was there, both mental and physical, which made Abby a woman worth getting to know much better.

He glanced at the clock on the back wall. Only a few more minutes until he could give up the pretense of accomplishing anything. Then he'd prepare for that romantic dinner with his wife. For months, he'd dreamed of a candlelit dinner with his fantasy lover. Those fantasies had nothing to do with the Abigail who'd spurned him because he'd barely known her. And, as it turned out, he hadn't really known Angelina at all even though he thought he had.

But none of that mattered because Angelina, Abigail and the woman he'd pledged to honor and cherish were three entirely separate entities. Now he relished the opportunity to uncover the layers hidden beneath his bride Abby's armor. Her eagerness to be alone with him and practice her gourmet cooking skills was touching. Yes, indeed. It promised to be an interesting evening. One he was suddenly anxious to get started. He checked the time again. Close enough, he'd decided. He put in enough overtime to justify leaving a few minutes early once in a while.

Prescott dropped his feet to the floor, then shrugged into his jacket. As he walked around to the front of his desk, he flipped through the reams of duplicate and triplicate papers stacked high in the In basket. He reached for the report he'd been working on, intending to add it to the stack, when he saw the letter from Abigail lying on the desk pad.

He'd be seeing his beautiful bride soon, sharing dinner, a bottle of wine and maybe something else... something that, in his opinion, was long overdue. He'd been very patient letting her get accustomed to her new life and recover from her illness. But every moment he was with her was becoming torture, and every night he had to struggle to keep on his side of the bed.

Absentmindedly tapping the letter to one end of the envelope, he ripped off a strip of paper and shook the letter out, allowing it to flutter to his desk. Curiously he unfolded it.

Her feminine script appeared to have flowed effortlessly across the page. Even though he'd never received an actual letter from her before, this brought back the excitement he used to get from her computer messages. Oh, how he'd lie in bed aching for her to be there with him after those long evenings of heated, innuendo-filled notes.

As Prescott read, anticipation turned to disbelief. Disbelief turned to anger. The letter was the typical "Dear John" variety, explaining that he just wasn't what she was looking for.

Betrayal—the feeling that was becoming all too familiar regarding Abby—stabbed him once again, this time in the heart rather than the back.

Prescott had cared for her then as Abigail and cared for her now as Abby. Why had she found him so unappealing as Bert, and yet so irresistible as Lobo that she'd flown thousands of miles to marry him sight unseen?

Was she incapable of making a commitment to a real flesh-and-blood man? Was this all some sort of game to her, a means of getting to Antarctica where she could make a name for herself in what she truly loved—her work? After all, she'd been spending long hours in the lab.

How could he have fallen victim to her wiles? How could he have assumed he knew the woman well enough to marry her? Meeting with her in person would have killed their romance in less than a fraction of a second. He would have realized she was incapable of loving him as he was, rather than who she'd fantasized him to be.

Prescott kicked himself for being a hundred kinds of romantic fool. He'd learned early enough in life that women couldn't be trusted. His mother had been a prime example. Obviously he had more of his father's blood than he liked to admit. All through the years of his wife's playing around, Jack Roberts had remained convinced she would settle down and they could all have a normal family life.

It had never happened. The last he knew, his mother was on husband number four and living somewhere in Switzerland. Worlds apart from him. Just like his own wife.

Prescott wadded the letter into a ball, then thought better of that and smoothed it out before burying it under a pile of folders. He strode from the office, yanking the door closed behind him. The glass rattled in its frame, alerting the lone secretary still on duty that Captain Roberts was *not* in a good mood.

"Everything okay, sir?" she ventured to ask.

"None of your damn business." He knew his clipped answer was rude, something the secretary wasn't accustomed to, but at the moment he didn't really care.

Pausing only long enough to shrug into his heavyweight green parka, he pushed open the door to the outside. The crisp Antarctic air did nothing to alleviate the anger directed both at himself and Abby.

He was a fool.

She was completely self-centered.

And at that particular moment, he couldn't decide which character flaw was worse. No matter what, he intended to have words with her as soon as both of them were in the privacy of their quarters. Then he'd put her on the first plane off the Ice.

He hoped he'd never have to see her again.

ABIGAIL SWEPT a cursory glance over the lab area, hoping that everyone had finally left. Getting two minutes of solitude on the sprawling continent was much more difficult than it should have been.

Seeing that all her colleagues had quit for the day, she sat at her assigned desk and took off the glasses she used for close-up work. She massaged the bridge of her nose, realizing there was no chance the night ahead would go as romantically as she had originally planned.

There was no way Prescott would have decided not to read the letter. And no way he wouldn't take it personally. Over the past week and a half since she'd recovered from the crud, they'd gotten along beautifully. Part of the reason was that neither had mentioned the circumstances that had brought them together; instead they'd focused on getting better acquainted.

Those same circumstances would now keep them apart. How would he be able to understand that she hadn't been attracted to Bert because she hadn't known him? No doubt it was a blow to his masculine pride that she had been so quick to fall in love with a stranger when she hadn't been able to spare any time for the same man in the flesh.

Abigail took off her lab coat and was hanging it on the hook beside the door when she noticed the letter she'd received today sticking out of the pocket. She'd been so concerned about how Prescott would react to her letter that she'd completely forgotten about her own mail. She slipped her glasses back on, then pulled out the envelope. Her eyes widened in surprise as she saw Bert's name and an unfamiliar Boulder post-office box number in the upper left-hand corner. What on earth could he have written to her about? Obviously it had been forwarded to her from BioGen after she quit.

She neatly sliced open the flap with a metal opener—anything to put off going back to the small room she shared with him and the inevitable confrontation. She read the note quickly. Shocked, she started over, taking time to absorb each numbing word. In his usual straightforward way, with not one word of apology, he'd broken off the relationship— or what might have become a relationship—between Bert and Abigail.

Abigail,

I hope this won't inconvenience you too much, but I won't be able to take you to the lecture as we planned. I'll be out of the country for an extended period of time by the night of our date.

I also hope you'll take this in the constructive manner in which it's intended, but you should consider signing up for some night classes on human relationships. I think you've been spending too much time burying yourself in your work. You have no idea how to treat other people, especially men.

When I first came to work at BioGen, I thought you'd be an interesting person to spend some time with. But after getting to know you a little better, I can understand where you got the nickname the Ice Queen.

Maybe someday you'll meet a man who will care enough to try to find a real woman beneath that frigid exterior. Until then, I wish you the best with your work.

Sincerely,
Bert

The words were clinically cold, unconscionably cruel. She'd felt bad about her letter until reading his. At least she'd tried to apologize. She'd been blunt but not vitriolic. He offered no such concessions, nothing conciliatory at all.

Anger surged through her. How dare he treat her this way? Ever since she'd arrived in Antarctica, he'd been playing the wounded victim. And he was just as guilty as she.

Abigail read the words once again, making certain she hadn't overreacted the first two times. She hadn't. With more calm and reserve than she was really feeling, she refolded the paper along the crisp line he'd apparently made with his thumbnail.

In fact, Prescott was *more* guilty than she. She had attempted to spare his feelings but he'd made no equal attempt. Why hadn't she seen that before now? She'd accepted his measured criticism, without shoving it back. Oh sure, she'd defended herself and her decisions, but not with as much vehemence as she now wished she had.

She might be guilty of two-timing Bert with a then-unnamed Prescott, but he'd added treachery and callousness to his list of crimes. And in her opinion, that was far worse than anything she'd said or done. How dared he call her frigid? How dared he suggest that she take night classes on human relationships?

Yes, dinner together tonight would be unusual. Abigail neatly placed her glasses in a case next to the papers she'd been working on, then grabbed the carefully folded note. After turning off the lights, she headed to the room she shared with her husband, rather, her ex-husband, as soon as that was possible.

This farce of a marriage had gone on far too long. After this latest insult, it would be impossible to make things work. She could no longer share the same room, closets, drawers, bathroom and especially bed with a man so heartless, especially since he obviously had such a low opinion of her. No wonder he hadn't attempted to make love to her. He thought of her as the Ice Queen. If she'd been in a better mood, she'd have seen the humor in that title. But, at the moment, all she could feel was the pain of his rejection.

She'd begun to see a glimmer of hope for them. Evidently the glimpse had been nothing more than a momentary lapse of good judgment, she realized wryly. She'd been showing a remarkable lack of logic for the past month, and it had finally caught up with her.

She stepped outside into the brilliant sunlight. She would never get used to the perpetual daylight. It was very disconcerting to leave after a full day's work and still have it as bright as it was when she'd arrived. Well, perhaps she would soon be back where the days were days, the nights were nights, and her life was predictable and totally under control again.

At their room, she started to slip the key into the lock, but stopped when Prescott called out, "It's open, darling."

The "darling" had more sarcasm in it than she'd ever heard before. Swallowing a sudden lump of trepidation, she entered the room. He lay on the bed, arms comfortably propped behind his head. He looked completely relaxed, a contrast to the way her insides were churning.

"How was your day, sweetheart?" he asked nonchalantly.

She closed the door and leaned against it for the few seconds it took to regain her composure. "I've had better."

"Yeah?" He shoved himself up. "So have I."

Abigail realized that before she met Prescott she'd never initiated a confrontation in her entire life. Even her sisters hadn't bothered arguing with her. But with Prescott it was becoming commonplace.

And she'd learned to hold her own. For mild-mannered Abigail, that was a real plus, especially if this new assertiveness could continue off the Ice and into her professional life.

"I promised you a glass of wine," he said, standing and making the distance between them shrink. But instead of walking all the way across to her, he stopped at his dresser and pulled out a bottle from an ice bucket. His actions unnerved her. He was too calm by far. If it wasn't for the hooded, guarded expression in his silvery blue eyes, she might have believed he hadn't read the letter, and he really meant for them to share a pleasant evening together.

With deft turns of the wrist, he twisted the corkscrew deep into the throat of the bottle. Inwardly she cringed, again realizing how little she really knew this man. "We need to talk," she said, holding up his letter to her.

"I couldn't agree more." He filled two glasses, picked up one, then stripped away the rest of the space separating them.

Abigail called on her anger. Yet as much as it burned inside her, she couldn't help but notice how handsome her husband was, how thoroughly male. How potently intriguing.

And dangerous.

"Your drink," he offered. Their fingers met, mingled. A spark, nothing to do with the anger, shot down her spine. His touch as he passed the glass felt warm, not at all hostile or remote. Not at all matching the expression in his eyes.

"Thanks."

"Drink up, *wife*. You may need it."

The unsubtle sarcasm in his tone gave life to her own animosity once again. If there was any fault, it belonged on both their shoulders. And Abigail didn't intend to forget it. She replied coolly, "It wouldn't hurt for you to take a good stiff drink yourself."

He quirked one brow. "Don't mind if I do."

When he turned to walk away, she felt a flood of relief. He disturbed her when he was so close. She just hadn't realized how much. Refusing to be caught in the corner again, she moved away, wine in one hand, letter in the other.

Prescott picked up his glass, then went to sit on the end of the bed, his long legs stretched out before him. Abigail remained standing, deciding any height advantage was an asset.

"Care to explain this?" she demanded, pressing the offensive. She casually sailed his letter onto the paisley-patterned bedspread.

"Sure." His easy compliance stunned her. But this attitude didn't last long. "Right after you're done explaining this." Prescott reached over to the nightstand and pulled out the letter she'd sent him from underneath a pile of folders. He stood, dwarfing her and stealing away her advantage. She suddenly felt overwhelmed. And, she hated to admit it, a strange rush of excitement.

"Where do you want to start?" He took a single step toward her. She sipped from her glass, taking a bigger gulp than she'd planned. The wine tingled warmly on the way down her throat.

"Why don't we start with arrogance?" He said the words softly, with a sensual slur. "Or maybe insincerity?"

"Arrogance?" she echoed. "Insincerity? *You* want to talk about those very unattractive traits, Captain? Well, so do I. We both received letters today. I agree we need to talk, but I expect you to do as much talking as listening."

Her vehemence seemed to surprise him. Good, she thought. Let it. His nasty little letter hurt. In the back of her mind, Abigail wondered if they'd ever stop hurting each other. One time, through the magic of computers, they'd been in love. Now all that seemed to remain was anger. And they both had plenty of it. Passionate, pained, frustrated anger.

Odd thing was, though, Prescott's eyes had a haunted expression, making him look every bit as hurt as she felt. Though she didn't want to be, Abby was touched. But there was still something about his attitude that kept her from softening.

He took a step closer and she forced herself not to flinch as he reached for her. His nostrils flared and Abby's heart pounded with a burst of fear at the passion in his eyes. Would he hit her? Or was he just trying to frighten her?

A muscle twitched in his jaw as he leaned toward her, his lips parted. Expecting more angry words, she was shocked when his mouth crushed down on hers.

Chapter Seven

His kiss tasted of passion, of possession.

Of anger.

Of promise. And pain.

A side of her personality she never knew existed surged to the surface. His fingers found her spine and she moaned as his strong, persuasive touch explored her back, her shoulders. This was the kind of excitement she'd dreamed of, wanted, the kind of thrill that kept her awake and warm at night. This was the kind of pleasure she'd always hoped she'd find in Lobo's arms.

Abby was becoming lost in the sensual onslaught. Pushing the confusion away, shoving away the betrayal and all the reasons she knew she shouldn't be with this man now, she surrendered to the dream.

His tongue met hers and Abby's knees grew weak. But he was there, offering physical support. And yet he kissed her with something else, as well, something more primitive. If it hadn't been for the intimate hours of computer correspondence, Abby realized she'd be experiencing fear right now. Prescott was angry, no doubt about that, but she didn't feel danger in his arms. At least, not the danger of being physically harmed.

His strong arms urged her closer, until their bodies were pressed tightly against each other. He deepened the kiss, demanding she respond to him, asking for her surrender. Instinctively she knew he wanted far more than she'd ever given a man before, far more than she'd given even him before. Opening her mouth for him, she offered herself. His heart pounded beneath her palm and she inhaled the scent of his masculinity. Abby realized now this was why she'd always held back with men. She'd been waiting for Prescott.

Slowly, he pulled away. She heard the ragged intake of his breath and felt her heart hammer in her chest. His hand still rested at the dip of her spine, but the charged air swirled around and between them. "That wasn't supposed to happen," he said, his voice taut.

"Don't apologize," she said softly, looking up at him. His lips were compressed tightly and he suddenly looked aloof. Prescott was obviously back in control of his emotions and she experienced a sense of longing, wanting him to let go again.

"I wasn't apologizing." As if realizing he still held her, Prescott jerked his hand away. The absence of his warmth was almost palpable. But even worse was the coldness in his eyes. "But I didn't intend for our *discussion* to degenerate into—"

"What?" she asked. "Into what, Prescott? A kiss? You can say it."

He looked surprised, but he couldn't have been more surprised than she. Abigail never acted so aggressively. But then again, nothing had been the same since she'd arrived on this frozen continent.

Abby tilted her chin defiantly, noticing that Prescott seemed every bit as bothered by what had just occurred as she was. He dragged his fingers through his hair, disturbing its golden blond neatness. She longed to do the same—to feel its silky texture against her skin.

He moved away, propping his hips against the dresser. She recognized the gesture as a way of putting both physical and emotional distance between them. Abby admitted to mixed feelings. She longed to stay in his arms, but was simultaneously glad for the gulf that separated them. It was much easier to cling to her anger that way.

"Look, Abigail—Abby." Prescott exhaled a deep sigh. Then he glanced uncertainly around the room, still raking his fingers through his hair as he did. Finally, the intensity of his gaze riveted her. "Getting physical's not going to solve anything."

Her body stiffened at the rejection in his tone. She struggled to pretend an indifference she truly didn't feel. An indifference she couldn't feel after what they'd just shared . . . a kiss that had started as punishment and ended in breathlessness, and with a hint of how things might be ... if only. Aloud she said, "I couldn't agree more."

He reached over and grabbed the letter she'd sent. She noticed the way his shirt stretched tightly across his chest and shoulders, accentuating the muscles in his arms she'd never noticed back home. Suddenly she was cognizant of the power Prescott possessed and the gentle way in which he'd touched her, despite his barely contained anger.

His fingers were white where they gripped the wrinkled, then obviously smoothed-out piece of paper. She barely suppressed a shudder and forcibly she reminded herself of his corresponding guilt. Breaking off her gaze, she bent to retrieve her own note.

"I think we need to talk this out," she said softly, hardly believing she spoke the words. "We acknowledge that we've both been hurt, but there's not much we can do about the past. We need to resolve to go forward."

"And where do you propose we go, Abby? I thought we *were* going forward. I thought I'd reconciled Abby and Angelina. Or do you have more nasty surprises for me? Any more letters that are going to end up on my desk when I start to believe you're going to be my wife, in every sense of the word."

"No more letters."

He folded his arms across his chest, yet his shoulders seemed to relax. Though she'd been grateful for the distance a few minutes ago, she wished that space didn't separate them. The room wasn't large, but the gulf was. When, after several minutes, he didn't make an effort to speak or to indicate forgiveness of any kind, she took the leap.

"It goes both ways," Abby said. "Do you have any more surprises for me?"

"None."

"Then?" she prompted.

"Then maybe there's nothing to talk about. Maybe we should accept that this just isn't going to work and call it quits. There doesn't appear to be any other choice."

In spite of her earlier anger, Abby's heart twisted. She wasn't ready to give up so soon. She still longed for the love she'd felt with Lobo. "There are always options. Surely your military training taught you that."

"It did. Sometimes a tactical retreat is the only option. Unfortunately, when you're as far from civilization as we are, there aren't any places to go. We're stuck. Together."

It all sounded so cold. And final. As if he was going to count the hours until she would be out of his life. "So we're back to the truce." Even as she said the words, Abby realized she didn't want a truce with her husband. She wanted something more. Passion. She'd never felt challenged by a man. Or protected. Or cared for.

Which was probably why she'd fallen for Lobo over a computer. Lobo wasn't safe, but he was strong and protective. He wasn't boring. He wasn't predictable. And these qualities had thrilled her. Abby was learning that what she had with her husband wasn't safe or predictable, either. So why didn't her heart pound with excitement rather than unease?

Because she was scared of opening up to him again. She'd tried it once, and he'd shot her down. She'd taken a chance and it had only caused her more pain.

As far as human relationships were concerned, he'd hit a nerve. Perhaps she wasn't as skilled at dealing with people as she was at delving into projects. And as far as romance went, she'd been half a pulse beat above comatose for her entire life. Lobo... and Prescott had brought her back to life.

"I'm not sure a truce will work. We've tried it once," he reasoned, his voice soft.

Deceptively soft, she thought. Prescott hadn't moved at all. He still stood across the room, his arms folded and his lips tight. She longed to see his expression brighten as he smiled at her. She wanted his eyes to light up the way they had this afternoon when she'd entered his office and he'd said he'd always have time for her.

"A truce is better than nothing. It's better than fighting and hurting each other."

"But what if a truce isn't enough for me? What if I want more from you?" He paused long enough so that the only sound she heard was the pounding of her heart. "What if I demand more than you're willing to give?" Her heart skipped several beats.

"Well, Angelina, how about it?"

"What are you suggesting?"

"That you be a wife." He hadn't moved, yet the air seemed instantly supercharged. Suddenly not nearly enough space separated them. Half the world wouldn't be enough at this moment. Be a wife? "My wife. In every way."

Abby felt her jaw drop.

Prescott pushed away from the dresser, advancing toward her slowly. She'd never considered herself a coward before, yet she retreated as far as possible. His steps were carefully measured, each footfall echoing in the stillness of the night. "I want you to be willing, Abby. I want you to surrender to me in a kiss of passion, not one of anger. And I want your surrender now."

"But we need to talk."

"Since you arrived here, talking hasn't been one of our greatest strengths. In fact, the only time we communicated effectively was over a computer linkup. We don't have a computer in here. It's just us—you and me."

Odd, she hadn't felt threatened when he'd reached for her earlier. Now, she did. His eyes were shaded by a lingering trace of hurt. Yet something else mingled there, something that intimidated her far more than the threat of an explosion.

He stopped, barely a few feet from her. He stood close enough for her to inhale the freshness of his scent. "I don't want a truce, Abby. It won't work for us. You know it as well as I do. Admit it. We've either got to go all the way or end this completely."

Not once had he raised his voice to her. There was no need. The man carried himself with military-style confidence and ease. Abby was glad Captain Roberts worked for the same country as she. But she couldn't admit that she believed he was right. A truce was what she needed in order to survive long enough to decide what she wanted to do. Abby shook her head. He was pushing too hard. He was blurring the lines between emotional and physical love.

"Go all the way?" she echoed weakly. Secretly, Abby realized if she made love with Prescott, she'd be lost, swept back into the fantasy of the perfect life she'd dreamed of with Lobo.

But her husband wasn't Lobo. Or rather, he was, with a dash of Bert the scientist and Prescott the officer tossed in. Abby wished she knew which personality was which. Or if the real man was a combination of all, which was another person entirely, a man she was only beginning to learn about.

"Do you want me to outline my terms, since I'm not prepared to accept yours?" he asked.

"What terms?"

He took another step. The back of her knees connected with the nightstand, effectively blocking any chance of her escape.

"The terms of your surrender, Abby."

"I'm not surrendering." The words didn't emerge with the strength she'd hoped.

"Oh, you will. Just as surely as I will. Like a good officer, I won't ask anything from you that I'm not willing to ask of myself."

"Never."

He laughed, a triumphant sound. "That's a long time, Abby."

Her instincts told her to run. But her common sense told her to stand and take him on his terms, but only after she got what she wanted, too.

"If we ever make love, Abby," he continued, "I promise it will be with your full cooperation and because you want it as badly as I do."

"You sound sure of yourself."

"I am. And just as sure of you. If Angelina wasn't a part of who you are—a big part of who you are—you would never have gotten on that plane with a promise to marry a man you'd never met. The fact you're still here listening instead of slapping my face, proves you've got the spirit and spunk I always saw there."

His forefinger stroked the length of her cheekbone, slowly, with a sensuality that almost made her forget their argument. "Do you like it when I do that?" He framed her face with his other hand, allowing his fingers to trace the outline of her ear and its sensitive lobe. "Or this?"

She debated how to answer. Wondered if she could still think straight.

"First, no more lies. No more secrets." He spoke near her ear, the warmth of his breath stirring the strands of dark hair curling around her neck.

With purpose, she tilted her chin back. Even that movement didn't quite make their gazes interlock. Abby wanted to read his expression and was frustrated by the fact she couldn't. "It goes both ways, Captain. No lies, no secrets from you, either."

"Done." His acquiescence was immediate, catching her off guard. "And to prove I mean it, I'll confess a secret I've been holding back." She waited tensely. "Ever since I first saw you at the lab in Boulder, I saw through your uptight ruse."

Abby shivered, even though the temperature remained steady. "It wasn't—"

"It was," he interrupted. Then he captured her chin between his fingers and tilted his own head forward so they had no option but to look at each other. "I saw a woman hiding behind glasses, a severe hairstyle and an oversize smock, smothering her femininity for the sake of appearing to be a serious scientist."

"I *am* a serious scientist," she protested.

"No argument from me there. You're one of the best." Again, the unsolicited compliment knocked her off balance. Not able to think of anything to say, she remained quiet. "But you're a woman who has wants and needs, and those shouldn't be sacrificed just for the sake of some image you think you need to project."

"That's a very typical male thing to say, Prescott. Unfortunately for women, most are judged on traits other than intelligence and work performance."

"Your achievements speak for themselves, Abby. Being beautiful isn't a detriment."

"Beautiful?" she echoed in disbelief.

He scooped up a handful of her hair and let it sift sinuously between his fingers. "Beautiful," he confirmed. "I tried to break through your barriers at work, but you wouldn't budge an inch."

"So you gave up and became Lobo and went looking for greener pastures," she said, not caring that her words held the sting she still felt. "I wasn't worth the effort." Abby wanted him to deny it. But she knew he couldn't.

"Look, I think we both went into this with expectations that may or may not be met. I respect you as a scientist, but I'll be honest and admit that I'm not sure how I feel about you as a wife."

"Well, Bert wasn't exactly the man of my dreams, either," she said, lashing back but instantly regretting the remark.

"Bert *is* me," he calmly reminded her.

Abby turned away, collected her wits, then continued, "Okay, I think we've established that we're both disappointed with the way things worked out. And I think that the quickest and easiest solution would be for me to leave on the next plane."

"That won't be for two more weeks."

If she'd cherished any hope that he'd beg her to stay, his terse comment effectively dashed it. "I can keep busy in the lab until then. My aquarium has stabilized so I can begin my study, the Japanese have requested my opinion on some data they collected on the ozone and there are dozens of reports of fossil discoveries I haven't seen before." She swallowed past the lump that had suddenly risen in her throat. "I can move into one of the dorms, too. I'll find someone who wouldn't mind having a roommate for a few days."

"You don't have to move out," he told her. "I think we could renegotiate our truce. Surely we can make it for a couple of weeks without killing each other."

"We're two adults. I think we should be able to manage that."

"Then I think there's only one way to seal our new peace treaty."

"How's that?"

"With a kiss. A kiss of honesty, nothing held back."

She trembled. Moving a step toward him, meeting him halfway, she rose to her tiptoes. Not to be outdone, Prescott also moved closer. When she leaned forward, trying to keep her hands at her sides to keep the kiss as impersonal as possible, he swept her into his arms.

Abby searched for all the honesty she possessed when her mouth opened and she accepted his tongue

with the passion he wanted, the passion she wanted.
From somewhere in the distance, she heard a moan
and didn't know whether the sound came from her or
her husband.

"EXCUSE ME, MRS. ROBERTS?"

It took Abby several seconds to realize the clerk was
trying to get her attention. Even though it had been
almost a month since her hollow wedding ceremony,
she still hadn't gotten used to answering to that name.
And it was just as well that she didn't since very soon
she would be taking her maiden name back. "Yes?"
she said, finally looking up. Abby took off her
glasses, blinked, then smoothed back the hair that
had tumbled around her shoulders.

"The captain wants to see you."

"Thanks. Tell him I'll be there in a few minutes."

The young man nodded, then left the lab.

Abby straightened on her stool, stretching the aching muscles of her back. She'd followed the terms of
their truce and had stayed out of his way as much as
possible. That meant spending most of her time in the
lab, in the mess hall or one of the clubs with her new
friends. And while it was nice to socialize and the
work was rewarding, she was pushing herself way too
hard. The physical strain combined with the emotional stress was beginning to wear her down.

She stopped in the rest room and freshened up before answering Prescott's summons. She'd already
worked a full day in the lab, not even stopping to eat

lunch. She hoped he wasn't going to initiate another argument because she simply didn't have the energy. In just two more days the plane that would take her out of his life forever was scheduled to arrive.

Things had been tense but quiet between them since they'd renegotiated the truce. Abby had accepted that there would be no stay of execution to keep her off that plane. At this point, all she wanted to do was leave without another ugly, painful confrontation.

Before knocking on his door, she unbuttoned her lab coat and took a deep, calming breath.

Prescott heard her knock, then called for her to come in. When she closed the door, he grinned a secretive grin.

"Have a seat." She perched on the edge of the chair facing his desk. "I've got a proposition for you. A professional proposition," he amended.

She leaned forward, encouraged by his light-hearted tone. "Tell me."

This time his grin was wry. "I wish my personal propositions got the same response from you."

"Prescott."

"All right, all right." He held up a hand. "I've got a-once-in-a-lifetime offer for you."

"Well?" she demanded. "Don't keep me in suspense."

"How would you like the opportunity to join me in setting up a study on pudgy penguins?"

"What?"

"It seems that the penguin population of the world is putting on weight. Some scientists are linking it with the global warming trend, which would allow the fish and krill that make up their food supply to thrive, thereby providing more food," he explained. "Anyway, they want someone to do the preliminary work, and I volunteered. And since you're interested in the ozone layer and its effects, I signed you up, too. That is, if you'd like to come."

Abby was delighted. She loved research and she loved animals... and she loved Prescott. Doing a study that combined all three would be more fun than work.

"I take it that look of rapture is an affirmative," he teased.

She nodded, then frowned. "But my plane leaves day after tomorrow."

"That's okay. They'll fly us there in a helicopter in the morning, we can tag penguins all day, then they'll come back for us in the evening. It'll be a long day, but we'll make it back in plenty of time for your plane."

Abby pressed her lips together to keep them from quivering. Her pleasure at being included in the project was tempered by the reminder that Prescott was waiting anxiously for her to leave.

She'd hoped they would settle back into some sort of comfortable companionship again. But since that last big confrontation, they'd been dancing around anything controversial. They'd both been very aware of an invisible line across which neither dared cross. And there had been no further attempts at intimacy and no talk about how to make the marriage work. Their new truce had truly been just that—a temporary peace treaty.

"I've got to get back to the lab," she said, suddenly anxious to get out of the room.

"Oh, and Abby," he called just as she reached the door. She stopped and glanced over her shoulder, expecting some sort of helpful reminder for her not to forget to pack an extra pair of socks or a notebook for the study. "I like your hair like that," he said and gave her a smile that could have melted the thickest iceberg... or the coldest heart.

Chapter Eight

Crystals of ice and a flurry of snow swirled around them as the helicopter lifted off the frozen surface. The pilot gave them a thumbs-up sign, then banked to the left and headed back toward McMurdo. Within seconds, the aircraft was just a tiny speck against the cloudless cerulean sky.

Abigail stood next to the small sled that would transport their supplies and stared at the helicopter until it disappeared completely. Slowly she pivoted, taking in the impressive and very desolate landscape, which stretched as far as the eye could see. And even more striking than the white, barren ground was the silence. It was absolute—so completely soundless that the quiet pounded in her ears like drums.

"Incredible, isn't it?"

She jumped at the burst of sound behind her and turned to see Prescott taking in the scenery with the same wonder that she was. "I never realized it would be so pretty. I guess I thought it would be just ice and snow like all the pictures I've seen. But I never took into consideration the way everything seems to sparkle or how amazing it looks when the green plants spring up as soon as the rocks warm up." She knelt and ran her fingertip lightly over the velvet-soft lichen.

"If you were staying longer, we could take a trip to Taylor Valley in the Dry Valleys. I hear the scenery is spectacular there."

Abigail glanced up, trying to read his expression, but he had his back to her as he began sorting through their supplies. Sometimes she thought she heard a note of regret in his voice that she was leaving. But if he didn't want her to leave, then why didn't he ask her to stay? Or at the very least, he could tell her he wouldn't mind if she stayed.

On the other hand, it was her decision to go, and why did it matter what Prescott thought about it? And would she change her mind if he did express some sort of interest in her remaining at McMurdo?

A gust of wind tugged at her fur-lined hood and she reached up with her gloved hand to hold it in place. If she were perfectly honest with herself, she didn't know what she would do. One minute she couldn't wait to get back to the real world and away from this pretense of a marriage. Then the next minute she would look at Prescott and her heart would skitter wildly in her chest as if she were a schoolgirl with her first crush.

"I could use a little help with this." His deep voice once again penetrated her thoughts.

Abigail blinked as she looked at his body, silhouetted against the ever-present sun as he bent over the pile of supplies. "Uh . . . sure," she said, hurrying to stand and busy herself with something that she hoped would keep her thoughts on the mission ahead instead of the man beside her.

They worked together, loading the sled with the equipment and personal items they'd brought. When it was balanced and secured with bungee cords, Prescott looped the towrope over his shoulder and called, "Ready?"

Abigail nodded and followed him as he started walking. "How do you know which way to go?" she asked, wondering how he could possibly get his bearings in a place with so few landmarks.

He held out his hand and she saw a small compass. "I *am* a trained military officer," he said, his tone dripping with cockiness. "I know what to pack."

Abigail didn't express her relief, but she felt her nerves relax. She didn't have any experience roughing it in the wilds of Boulder, much less out here in the middle of nowhere. It was very comforting to be with a man who obviously knew how to handle the situation.

The sled glided across the slick semifrozen earth and Abigail had to lengthen her strides to keep up with Prescott. When he saw how much effort it was taking her, he slowed. "Sorry about that." His smile was warmer than the weak summer sun high overhead. "I'm used to people keeping pace with me, but they go on double-time marches as a matter of routine."

The air was so thin and cold she was having trouble filling her lungs fast enough. She barely managed a weak, appreciative smile as his boots squished in the soft snow in a cadence slow enough for her to walk beside him.

As they climbed a gentle rise, the ground showed no evidence of human trespass. In fact, it would be easy to pretend that they were the first people to travel through this area. When they reached the rounded summit and looked down over the other side, it was as if they were discovering a new world.

"Now I know how Admiral Byrd must have felt," Prescott commented, echoing her thoughts with an intuitiveness that often popped into their conversations. It was odd the way their thoughts paralleled. "I've always wished I'd been an explorer."

"Scientists are contemporary explorers," Abigail commented. "In our own way, we're searching unexplored territory and discovering new frontiers."

He nodded thoughtfully. "Yes, you're right. Maybe that's why I love the research element of my work rather than the actual application. I've considered going to medical school, but it just didn't hold the appeal that working on different scientific projects does." He consulted his compass and unfolded a map. "I think the rookery is just over the next hill."

"At least the trip down will be easier than the one coming up." Her gaze drifted to the sled, then rose to his face. She was not surprised to see a twinkle in his blue eyes that probably matched the anticipation in her own.

"It's been years since I went sledding," he remarked as if reading her mind.

"Me, too."

They both glanced back down at the sled. "I'm game if you are," he challenged.

"You first," she returned.

"Oh no. We'll go together."

"But what about the equipment?"

"You can hold it on your lap. Besides, there's nothing sensitive or breakable and it's packed well. Even if it falls off, it would be into soft snow, so there's no way it'll get damaged."

She figured he knew more about their load than she did, so she nodded. "Okay, then let's do it."

He unfastened the bungee cords and helped her settle on the front half of the sled, then nestled the two duffel bags between her legs. "Ready?" he asked.

She grinned and he positioned himself on the back of the sled. The small size of the vehicle forced them into the most intimate position of their entire relationship as he wrapped his legs around her and snuggled against her back. Even though they were separated by several layers of very thick clothing, Abigail could feel his heartbeat and the heat of his body as it molded to hers. His arms circled her waist as his hands held the rope in front of her.

Abigail turned her head to tell him she was ready, but instead, her open mouth brushed over his. Startled at the contact, they froze, their gazes locked and the misty fog of their warm breath mingled in the frigid air. Slowly the space disappeared until his lips touched hers, tentatively, tenderly. It was cold outside, but as the embrace became heated, it chased the chill away.

Her eyelids drifted closed and her head tilted back to accommodate his height advantage. His hand, gloved in soft leather, cupped her cheek as his mouth moved over hers with increasing ardor until he reluctantly pulled away. For another long, meaningful moment, neither moved but continued to look questioningly into each other's eyes.

"Mmm...I guess we'd better get going," she said, more to break the pounding silence than to actually shatter the mood.

"Yes, I suppose so." His voice was ragged and he cleared his throat before adding, "Hang on tight."

Since the bags offered no security, she leaned back against the strength of Prescott's chest and held on to his legs. She knew these were not the actions of a woman who was counting the hours until she would be leaving this man behind, probably forever. But she marked her behavior off to Antarctic insanity. As soon as she got back to the U.S., her logic and common sense would return and she could go on with her life. The first thing she'd do would be to cancel her membership in CompuLink.

Before she could make any more plans, Prescott pushed off and the sled answered the call of gravity and slid down the hill. Gradually it picked up speed until the wind tugged Abigail's hood off and numbed her cheeks and lips with its biting chill. The bottom rushed toward them and she braced herself for a tumble. But just as they bounced over the last icy bump, Prescott tightened the rope and kept the nose of the sled up so it crunched to a smooth stop.

The excitement of the ride and the relief that they'd survived it unscathed brought forth a burst of laughter. Abigail looked into Prescott's handsome face and knew her own cheeks must be just as red as his. A dusting of ice frosted his hair and clung to his thick, dark brown lashes. Suddenly the laughter caught in her throat and she felt the sting of tears at the thought that after tomorrow she'd never again see that face now so familiar and dear to her.

Abruptly she turned away and climbed off the sled, then busied herself repacking the duffels. Prescott must have understood, or at least recognized her confusion, because he didn't comment but merely pitched in to help with the load, then looped the rope over his shoulder.

The next hill was higher than the last and it took all their energy to reach the top. Abigail was relieved at the excuse not to make conversation, because at the moment, her thoughts were more jumbled and confused than they'd ever been.

They struggled to the summit, and the sight below took away what little breath they had left. In the distance, a large body of water stretched to the horizon. At least a half mile from shore where the water was mostly clear, a weathered, decrepit-looking trawler flying a Russian flag coasted slowly along, dragging its nets. A flock of gulls followed closely, dipping down for a free meal when a fish ventured too near the surface.

Chunks of ice had broken off the ice shelf and were slowly floating away to sea while hundreds of fat, sleek penguins played games of tag, leaping off and back onto the icebergs. The noise of their chirping and splashing filled the air, creating a raucous contrast to the absolute silence on the other side of the hill.

"How many are we supposed to document?" she asked.

"As many as possible, but they're hoping for at least fifty to legitimize the study." He studied the area, then indicated a circular route with a gradual descent to the frozen beach. "I think we should go that way to keep from disturbing them as much as possible."

Abigail agreed and let Prescott lead. When they got to the base, they took a quick lunch break and devoured the sandwiches and potato chips the cook had packed for them. By moving slowly and unaggressively, they were able to get within a few feet of the hole the penguins were using to gain entrance to their underwater feeding area and playground.

As she and Prescott set up the scales and unpacked the tagging equipment, Abigail was distracted by the antics of the penguins. Instead of crawling out of the water and slithering onto the ice as a seal or walrus would, these aquatic birds rocketed out of the hole, shooting several inches higher out of the water than necessary before landing on their bellies and sliding across the ice. They scrambled to their feet, then began waddling awkwardly around, having immediately lost their gracefulness once they stood on land.

Prescott said, practically shouting above the noise, "During the winter, they stay on the pack ice, then travel south to here. The males arrive a few days before the females and pick out the nesting sites. From the way they're acting, the females must have just arrived and the courtship ritual is in full blast. Our timing is perfect. We wouldn't have wanted to disturb them after they'd already begun laying their eggs."

"Their nests will be in the rocks, won't they?"

Prescott nodded. "They'll use smaller pebbles to build their nests, then the bigger rocks will protect them from snowdrifts and wind."

Abigail looked around at the birds as their heads bobbed up and down and the males danced around the females of their choice.

"They look pretty silly, don't they?" Prescott commented rhetorically.

But Abigail laughed as she answered, "It's just as it should be. Men in the human kingdom have it way too easy. All they have to do is call up on the telephone, then show up at the restaurant. Women will meet them there and even pay the bill."

"It's called paying for the pleasure of our company," Prescott teased.

"Well, the penguins have a better system," Abby noted. "Not only do the males fawn all over the females, but they split the work by helping build the nests and sitting on the eggs half the time."

"The emperor penguin dads are even more helpful," Prescott added, "because they sit on the nest almost the entire incubation period. When they get bored, they carry the eggs on the tops of their feet and waddle over to the other fathers-to-be. They all put their eggs in the middle so they can keep them warm while they visit, then they take their eggs and go home."

Abby laughed at the mental image of a fat penguin balancing an egg on his feet as he walked.

By offering a smelly, but obviously tempting morsel of fish to the penguins, Prescott was able to begin the process of catching them. One by one, they were weighed, measured, then tagged with small, bright yellow numbered bands around one of their legs. Abigail logged each bird's information in a notebook while Prescott released one creature and caught another.

They worked together efficiently and cheerfully, not stopping for a break until the greedy penguins began coming back for seconds and Prescott began having to spend time sorting through the ones already tagged and those that hadn't been documented yet.

"I think we should move farther down the shoreline," he said. "These are all Adélies, and I'd like to find a few other species of penguins to include in the study. I doubt we'll run into any rock hoppers or macaronis, but there might be a few emperors in the area."

Abigail finished making notations in the log, then carefully stowed it inside one of the waterproof duffels. "Probably not. We've caught thirty-seven penguins here—"

"So it would be a good idea to find a different rookery."

Abigail helped him reload the equipment. The penguins, momentarily disappointed at losing the source of their free meal, soon turned their attention back to the ceremony of mating. Their calls and whistles were audible for several minutes as the two scientists left the site to follow the curve of the coastline around the rocky hill. Just as Prescott had predicted, there was another rookery in the process of being reinhabited, and he and Abby quickly set up the equipment again and returned to work.

They had tagged and documented another dozen birds when a blast of wind nearly ripped the pages out of the logbook. Abigail had to close it quickly to protect their work. She glanced up at the sky, surprised to notice that the sun was completely obscured by a layer of thin gray clouds. "We'd better get packed. If those clouds mean the same thing they mean back in Colorado, we're going to get some snow," she said, struggling to smooth the creased and folded pages of the book without having the wind tear them out completely.

Prescott looked at the sky and frowned. "It doesn't look good, does it?" He finished fastening the tag on the last penguin, then gently set him free.

But even though they hurried, the storm moved more quickly, and snow was already pelting them by the time the equipment was reloaded and they were heading back to the helo pad. A thick, cold fog settled in, bringing on the first semblance of twilight she'd seen since she arrived.

Prescott had to stop next to a medium-size boulder so he could find some shelter from the wind long enough to call the base on the portable radio from their pack. After a brief, static-plagued, shouted dialogue, he snapped the antenna down and returned the radio to its case. "He's not coming," Prescott announced solemnly, obviously trying not to show his reaction to the news.

"What do you mean, he's not coming?" Abigail yelled into the wind, not making any attempt to hide the rising panic she was feeling. "Somebody has to pick us up. Who knows how long this storm will last, and we can't stay out here in the middle of it. We'll freeze to death. We're not prepared for this—"

"Calm down," he interrupted, obviously aware she was on the verge of hysteria. Prescott reached into his deep parka pockets and pulled out a map. "The pilot said there was a Russian weather station near here. He didn't think it was occupied this summer. All the nations here on Antarctica have an agreement that in times of emergency, we can take shelter in their facilities. So that's where we'll spend the night."

"Spend the night?" she echoed. "But my plane leaves tomorrow—"

"Relax," he said, his eyes chilling to several degrees colder than the freezing air around them. "You'll make it back in time for your plane. I know how anxious you are to get away from here. If the weather's too bad for the chopper, surely it's too bad for the plane, so the flight should be delayed for several days."

Abigail shivered, not from the rapidly dropping temperature, but from the icy blue of his eyes. She hadn't meant it to sound that way, but she realized it must have seemed as if she was devastated at the thought of missing her flight. Actually, after the last few days, especially today when they'd worked together so well, she wasn't as anxious to leave as she had been when she'd declared her intentions. Even then, she hadn't wanted to leave so much as she'd been frightened by her own feelings and the possibility of being hurt. He'd pressed the issue and she'd called his bluff. But his reaction, or lack of reaction, had locked her into leaving. It was more of a planned escape to save her pride, rather than an exit *away* from Prescott.

And she couldn't really back down now without examining her feelings and trying to explain them. Since she still felt as insecure as she had then, she dared not open herself up for that sort of rejection. Instead she forced her stiff lips into a brave smile and said, "Okay, then let's try to find this Russian sanctuary before our vital body parts freeze off."

Prescott consulted his map and compass, fighting the wind and snow for a couple more minutes before he turned and headed inland. The wind was whipping from every direction, so much of the time they were walking directly into it. Just as Abigail's face began feeling unbearably numb, they topped a hill and looked down on the most welcome sight she'd ever seen.

The Russian weather station was barely visible between the driving sheets of snow. It stood in the middle of a flat valley. A dull metallic brown building, surrounded by dozens of antennae and measuring devices mounted on poles, it looked small and abandoned, but solid.

"Home sweet home," Prescott remarked wryly. "After what we've been through, it looks pretty good to me." After giving her a relieved thumbs-up sign, he changed the rope to his other shoulder, then bent into the wind as they began their descent. As if it knew they were headed for shelter, the sled threatened to pass them on a downward trek of its own. Prescott had to struggle to keep it under control until they reached the station.

His gloved hand slid uselessly on the frozen latch and he had to pound it with his fist to break the ice before he was able to open the door. He staggered inside, not caring how much snow he tracked on the floor as he pulled the sled in behind him. Abigail stood outside, alternately annoyed at his ungentlemanly entrance and relieved that she hadn't had to enter first.

"Good grief!" she exclaimed after joining him inside the tiny room. "It's colder in here than it is outside. And it's dark."

"Gripe, gripe, gripe," Prescott mumbled as he took out a flashlight and swept the wide beam around the room.

Abigail realized she wasn't being a very good sport about the whole situation, even though it was obviously not his fault. No wonder he wanted her to leave. He thought he and the wild, sexy Angelina would be having a great adventure before settling down to raise a family, when in fact he'd found himself shackled to a wimpy woman who'd complained about almost everything from the moment her boots touched the ice.

Well, she resolved, she could at the very least make her last hours—or days, as the case might be—as pleasant as possible. Perhaps, when she had gone, he would regret it, instead of feeling only relief that he was free again.

She sucked in a deep breath of the stale, frigid air and swallowed back a cough. A match scraped and a warm golden glow spread throughout the room, lighting all but the darkest corners. Prescott replaced the globe on the oil lamp and set it on the table.

"Homey, huh?" he remarked as they surveyed their lodgings. A large wood stove dominated one corner of the room, proving by its size that it was the most valuable piece of furniture in the room. A desk took up most of the wall beside the door and the table was pushed against the opposite wall. Wedged into the remaining space was a single cot, which obviously doubled as a couch.

"As soon as we get the stove lit, it'll be great." Abigail was trying to be optimistic, but when Prescott gave her a skeptical look, she amended, "Well, maybe not great. But at least warm. And brighter. All right, brighter."

He didn't answer, but turned his attention to building a fire in the stove. Abigail stood transfixed by the sight of him as the lamplight turned his hair into a spun-gold halo. Her fingers tingled inside her gloves, longing to touch its softness. When he stood to reach for the matches on a high shelf, his tall, muscular body seemed to fill the small room.

Abigail's gaze drifted back to the small cot. Small room. Small bed. Small amount of time left as Mrs. Prescott Roberts.

Yes, tonight might be her last chance.

Chapter Nine

"I don't know about you, but I'm starving." Prescott gave the stove one last threatening look that dared it to go out, then dusted the cinders and wood chips off his hands. "These penguin roundups sure do work up a fella's appetite."

"I guess you had your chance to play cowboy today, didn't you?"

"Yep, and now you have your chance to dazzle me with your gourmet cooking skills." He pulled a chair close to the stove and extended his hands and feet toward the radiating heat.

She gave him a stricken look and appeared to be on the verge of breaking into tears. Boy, he'd heard about women and their rapidly changing moods, but he'd never spent much time around females, so he hadn't known just how mercurial they could be. Just when he thought he was figuring her out, she did something totally out of character.

But then, that was the whole problem with their relationship, wasn't it? Being out of character was the norm since neither knew being *in* character required some sort of insight into that person.

"What's wrong, Abby?" he dared ask.

Her fingers fumbled as she took off her gloves and held her hands over the stove. "I can't exactly cook," she admitted.

"But you said—"

"No," she corrected. "*Angelina* said she could cook. *I* can't. All those heat-and-eat meals we've been cooking over your hot plate are about as gourmet as I get."

He wanted to ask her if *anything* she'd told him on the computer was true, but he decided there was no sense in starting an argument. The cabin was too small and their time together was too short. "Okay, we'll *both* cook," he conceded. "So, what did you bring for dinner?"

"What do you mean, what did I bring for dinner?" she asked. "I packed the lunch and you packed the food for dinner, right?"

"Wrong." He shook his head emphatically. "I thought *you* were taking care of the food since I was handling the other supplies."

"I had no idea we were going to be spending the night out here in the wilderness."

"Well, one of the first rules of venturing out of camp is to be prepared for *any*thing," he commented.

She turned to him, hands planted on her hips, and stared at him accusingly. "*You're* the grown-up Boy Scout. I was never even a Brownie. I never started a campfire or sold a cookie or anything. How on earth am I supposed to know anything about packing for a camping trip that wasn't supposed to be a camping trip?"

He threw up his hands in resignation. Okay, he had to take at least some of the responsibility for not being prepared, but he didn't want to give her any further ammunition. Instead he tried to steer the conversation around to a more positive vein. "Never mind whose fault it is. The bottom line is that we're stuck here at least for tonight and neither of us brought any food." He glanced over at the closed cabinets over the sink. "Surely the Russians have some sort of goodies stashed here."

Behind one door was a collection of first-aid supplies and replacement parts for all the equipment outside the station. The next cabinet contained a couple of unmatched gloves, four paperback books printed in Russian, some kitchen utensils and some supplies for recording the weather data. And last but not least, on a shelf next to a box of candles, there were a dozen square cans.

"I can't tell by the labels, but I think they're some sort of food," Prescott said, studying the baffling symbols on the paper wrappers. He could read and speak a half dozen languages. Unfortunately, even though he'd been stationed there briefly, Russian wasn't one of them.

Abigail took a good look at one of the cans, then shook it while listening to its contents shift inside. "I don't know what it is, but I agree that it might be something to eat." She glanced around with an apprehensive expression.

Prescott couldn't help but think that even with a smudge of charcoal across one cheek and shadows of exhaustion under her midnight blue eyes, he found her incredibly appealing. Perhaps it was her strong, but very feminine features or the fact that he knew there was an impressive brain behind all that beauty. Whatever the reason, he had to admit that she fascinated him. He didn't know if their marriage would last for another month, but he did know that he didn't want her to be on that next plane to New Zealand.

"After all, they are unwittingly providing us a place to get out of the weather and sleep," Abigail continued, unaware of his rambling thoughts. "Do you think it might cause some sort of international incident if we were to eat their food, too?"

"No, I doubt it. It's all part of the same unwritten policy that everyone shares everything but their technology. And sometimes even that. I guess because we're just a small group here on such a large, isolated place that we can all work together. It boils down to survival being the most important thing."

Her stomach chose that moment to give a most unfeminine growl and she gave him a sheepish smile. "You're the highly trained military professional. Don't you have one of those handy-dandy pocket-knives that has everything from a toothpick to a chain saw?" she asked, staring at the cans with an intensity bordering on obsession. "We've *got* to get these opened."

Prescott almost hated to admit it since she seemed to find humor in his Boy Scout nature, but he did indeed have a Swiss army knife in one of his pockets. And while the chain saw was an exaggeration, the small utensil had a dozen assorted blades and handy tools. He reached into this pocket for the knife and flipped out the can-opener attachment. He noted the smile twitching at the corners of Abby's full lips, but she wisely remained silent.

It took a lot of coordination, punctuated with a few grunts and muffled curses, to dig through the metal, but finally he lifted the lid with undisguised triumph. "Ta-da . . . dinner is served."

Abigail looked at the congealed substance with suspicion. "What is it?"

He sniffed it and was barely able to keep from shuddering. Then he flipped out a fork, which he thrust into the contents of the can. He meant to chip off a piece. Instead, the entire substance stuck together as he pulled. With a disgusting slurp, the meat slid out and perched in an unappetizing lump on the end of the fork. Bravely he nibbled on one corner.

"Hmm...yum...it's the Russian equivalent of our pork adobo," he announced.

Abigail's lip curled and her nose wrinkled involuntarily. But she managed a shaky, if insincere smile. "Maybe it'll taste okay if we warm it up. Can you hold it over the flame?"

He did as she suggested, and they stood side by side and watched the gelatinous substance around the meat warm, then drip into the flames with a crackling hiss. "Did you see any plates?"

Abigail returned to the cabinets and dug through the miscellany until she found two metal plates and two twisted forks. "I think Uri Geller must have been here," she commented wryly as she tried to bend the misshapen tines back into place.

"Maybe he's the one who ate the good food." Prescott plopped the partially charred meat onto one of the plates. When he started to divide it evenly, Abigail hurried to stop him.

"I wasn't as hungry as I thought," she assured him. "You did most of the work, so you deserve most of the food."

"Coward," he responded, not the least bit fooled by her burst of generosity. "I'm a nineties man and I believe in splitting everything fifty-fifty."

Abigail rummaged in her parka pocket and pulled out an opened roll of Certs. "That's okay. I think I'll diet tonight and just have these."

"You have Certs!" Prescott exclaimed. "And you didn't tell me. You were just going to eat them all and not share!"

"Calm down. You can have half. Jeez, what a whiner," she muttered, but there was an amused twinkle in her blue eyes. Carefully she peeled off the outer wrapper and placed the Certs on their plates one at a time with a resounding clink. "One for you...one for me...one for you...one for me..."

He glanced at the sizzling meat mess rapidly cooling on the plate and realized how ridiculous this whole conversation was sounding. On the other hand, he felt closer to Abby than he'd felt since their first face-to-face meeting. As she looked up at him, there was a vulnerability in her expression he'd never seen before. "Now that you've fixed dessert, do you think you could find us something to drink?" he asked. "There's nothing left in our thermos, is there?"

Abby shook her head. "We didn't bring much," she reminded him. She found a coffeepot on the shelf over the stove, then headed for the door. Outside, the wind whistled around the corners of the small building and piled snow up against the windows. As she opened the door, the heavy plank of wood almost shoved her against the wall when the wind grabbed it. Prescott strode over and took the pot from her hands.

"I'll get the water, er, snow." He leaned out of the cabin to get some clean, pure snow and filled the pot. "Since the water content is so much lower here, it's going to take a lot of snow to get enough water for a cup of coffee. Back in Colorado it's about seven inches of snow for an inch of water, but here it's about thirty for one.''

"Since we're in the coldest, driest spot on earth, I suppose that's to be expected," she commented, her voice muffled as she knelt on the linoleum floor and peered under the sink in her search for coffee grounds.

Another blast of wind shook the cabin. "And the windiest," he added.

There was a rattle and clatter as she moved things around, followed by a disappointed grunt. "There's nothing under here to drink but this." She backed out and held up an unopened bottle of vodka.

"That'll have to do, I guess," Prescott commented. "I've always heard that Russian vodka is the best." He gingerly chipped off a chunk of the canned meat and speared it with his fork. "Maybe it'll make this taste better than it looks."

Abby obviously wasn't convinced that was possible, but she screwed off the top and set the bottle on the table. They still had a couple of paper cups left and she placed them ceremoniously above the plates. "Dahling, would you care to pour?" she asked in an exaggeratedly cultured drawl.

"No, dearest, you go ahead," he answered, picking up the accent. "I'm busy carving the bird...or is this the beef? Well, whatever it is, I'm carving it." He sliced off a ragged chunk. "And to think I complained about pork adobo."

Her lovely, full lips curved into one of the few genuine smiles he'd witnessed, and it took his breath away. God only knew how she would affect him if she turned the full power of her feminine charms on him.

Without further preliminaries, he opened his mouth and put the bite of meat inside. Slowly he chewed and his expression changed from anxiety to surprise. "Hey, it's not half-bad."

"Really?"

"I wouldn't lie to you about something as important as food." His gaze lifted and met hers across the table. Suddenly his tone sobered. "In fact, I wouldn't lie to you about anything. My biggest sin is that I didn't tell you the whole truth."

Her eyes softened. "Neither of us did."

"Too bad we couldn't start over... from the very beginning." The words sounded innocent enough, but he felt his breath catch in his lungs as he waited for her response. Now that he'd said it, he realized it was what he wanted most in the whole world. In spite of all the lies and misunderstandings, he wished they could both take back all the nasty things they'd said to each other and begin afresh.

To his vast relief, she smiled. "I don't think it's too late." As if to demonstrate her new cooperative spirit, she took a bite of the meat. "You're right," she agreed. "It's better than it looks." She picked up her paper cup of vodka and held it toward Prescott. "To us... a new beginning."

"To détente, Antarctica style," Prescott added and tapped his cup carefully against hers.

Their eyes remained locked as they sipped the vodka. By the time the meat was finished, half the bottle's contents had mysteriously disappeared.

"So, comrade, how was dinner?" he asked as they lounged back in their chairs, crunching on their Certs as if they were rare delicacies.

"Umm..." she answered, pausing to think of the appropriate word to describe their meal. "Unique."

He tipped a little more liquid into their paper cups before commenting as casually as he could, "So you're anxious to get home, huh?"

Abby hesitated for a moment, her cup halfway to her mouth. "Yeah, I guess so. But I think I'll take the scenic route."

"You mean the New Zealand–Australia-Tahiti-Hawaii flight?"

"That's the one." Abby's expression darkened. Such a schedule should have brightened her spirits instead of making her sad.

"If you take your time traveling, we might reach home about the same time." He sneaked a glance in her direction to catch her reaction.

"You're going back to Boulder?" Her head snapped up at the news.

"Thought I might. I like Boulder."

Abby watched him through slightly narrowed eyes. "So do I. But I'd like to find a new job. I feel stifled at BioGen. Will you go back to work there?"

"No, my assignment is finished with them. But I've been rootless for a long time. Maybe I should settle in one spot, you know, have a base. It all depends on a lot of things."

"Like what?"

"Oh, I doubt that you'd be interested in my plans." Prescott casually picked up the plates and took them to the sink.

"Of course I'm interested," Abby protested. "After all, we're married . . . well, sort of."

"But not for long, right?" He knew he was treading on thin ice, but he simply couldn't stop the direction of the conversation. "I suppose an annulment will be the first thing on your agenda when you get back."

"I suppose so. Not that there's really any rush."

"You mean you're not in a hurry to get free so you can go husband-hunting on the computer right away?" He opened the door again, scooped up some snow on one of the plates, then scrubbed it with a little more force than necessary.

Abby jumped to her feet so abruptly that her chair teetered over backward. "I was *not* husband-hunting!"

"You could have fooled me. You sure took me up on my offer fast enough."

"That was because I fell in love with—with you," she said softly.

"With me? Hardly. You fell in love with Lobo."

"You *are* Lobo." She sat back down and stared at the tabletop. "You *were* Lobo."

"And you were Angelina."

"And now we're just Prescott and Abby, trying to get to know each other better."

He searched her face for any sign that she was joking or playing him for a fool. Instead he saw only the shine of tears glistening in her dark blue eyes and a shaky smile begging to be encouraged lingering on her lips.

"Abby..." he whispered.

"Yes?"

Never had he wanted to take her into his arms more than he did at that moment. But he hesitated, afraid to push too hard. "It's getting late," he said, substituting that impersonal comment for what he really wanted to say.

"What time is it?" she asked, her own voice unsteady as if she didn't quite know what to talk about, either.

He pushed up the sleeve of his sweater and looked at his watch. "Twenty-one hundred hours."

"Nine o'clock." She glanced at the milky light still peeping around the closed shutters. "This constant daylight is driving me crazy," Abby murmured. "What do you want to do now?"

"Do you mean now like tonight or now like for the rest of our lives?"

"I mean tonight."

"Well, the possibilities are endless, aren't they," he responded lightly, trying to change the mood back to their earlier camaraderie. "We could tell ghost stories or sing campfire songs...or maybe we could just go to bed and—"

"Talk," she interrupted uneasily. "Yes, we definitely need to talk. About work. You know, the penguin project. Let's go over the plans again. What do we do next?"

"What's the matter? Are you a little nervous about going to bed with me?" Prescott took another swallow of vodka, then sat down on the cot and leaned against the wall, looking Abby over from head to toe.

"Of course not. We've been sleeping together since I got here...sort of," she returned.

"Sleeping is certainly the right word, isn't it?" He leaned forward and held out his hand to her. "Come and sit down, Abby. I won't bite. At least I haven't so far." He moved a pillow and discovered a pack of cards. Curious, he opened the box, took out the deck and shuffled it with deft hands. "Tell you what, let's play a game of cards."

Obviously relieved, she jumped at the distraction. "Good idea. What kind? Gin?"

"Do you know how to play poker?"

"I've played some." Abby found a box of wooden matches, came over and sat beside him on the small bed. "What kind of poker?"

"Strip?" he suggested innocently.

"Are you out of your mind?" Abby scooted to the far end of the bed.

"Relax, Abby. It's a new kind of strip poker." He cut the cards and spread them neatly across the bed with a flair that any Las Vegas dealer would envy.

"Strip poker is strip poker." She crossed her arms firmly across her chest, her body language speaking more loudly than words.

Prescott waggled his eyebrows at her. "In this form of strip poker, you keep your clothes on. Whoever wins a hand gets to *imagine* taking an item of clothing off the loser. Anyway, it's too cold to play the other way. I wouldn't want you to get chilled."

Abby relaxed slightly. "Actually I'm feeling a lot warmer than I was an hour ago."

"A half bottle of vodka will do that for you."

She sat up straighter as a new thought hit her. "And why are you automatically assuming that I'm going to lose?"

"Hey, what difference does it make? We'll kill some time, have some fun, and you can keep your clothes on. Perfectly innocent." He moved to sit cross-legged at the end of the bed.

Abby turned until she faced him from the opposite end and did likewise. "Deal the cards."

"We need to ante up. I'm putting in two matches."

"Fine. Me, too. What's the game?" Abby pushed up the sleeves of her sweater.

"Five card stud." Prescott dealt the first hand. He picked up his cards and frowned as he looked at the odd symbols marking the face cards. "Do you suppose the one with the beard is a king?"

"Aha. Now I know you have at least one king."

"Maybe I'm bluffing."

"Yeah, right. And maybe Domino's Pizza is on its way to deliver a large pepperoni deluxe to our door." She sorted through her cards, meticulously moving them from one spot to another before finally looking up to meet his gaze and smiling.

"How many do you want?"

"I'll keep these," she replied.

He didn't know whether to worry or laugh at her show of confidence. Another glance at his own cards confirmed that even though he couldn't read the letters he could count the shapes, and he had nothing even close to making a winning hand. He tossed three down and dealt himself three more—three that were no better than the first ones. "Dealer calls."

"Does that mean I show you my cards?"

He smiled. Ahhh...this could prove to be more fun than he'd imagined. "Yes, you show me yours and I'll show you mine."

She spread them out in front of him and he groaned. "I'm not sure what it's called, but I think it's good," she said.

"It's called a full house," he informed her as he looked at her three tens and two fours. "And it beats my nothing. Okay, what do I take off?"

"Your—" she gave him a teasing look, then finished with "—sweater."

"Okay," he said, and pulled the cable-knit wool garment over his head.

"Hey, I thought you said we'd *imagine* taking things off," she reminded him hurriedly.

"Yes, I did. But it *is* getting hot in here. That stove really can heat this room."

"Oh." She didn't seem to be entirely satisfied with the explanation, but was getting caught up in the spirit of the moment. "Is it my turn to deal?"

He handed her the cards and she fumbled her way through a messy shuffle, then dealt them five cards each. They went through the process of betting, discarding, adding cards and increasing the bet. This time, Prescott was pleased to end up with two pairs that were good enough to win the hand.

"Hmm, what do I want?" He looked her over from head to toe, letting his gaze linger suggestively on certain strategic feminine spots. Finally he said, "A sock, I think."

"A sock? I thought you'd go for the big time. Like my sweater, at least."

"Disappointed? I happen to think you have very sexy feet, Abby. They're so slim and have such a nice arch. And toes made for kissing. Besides, your socks are so long. I actually get to undress you all the way up to your knees. In my mind, of course." He gave her a beguiling smile and she shifted uncomfortably. "Wow...your feet are even more beautiful than I remembered."

"Deal the damn cards," she muttered.

He scooped up the cards from the bed, shuffled them smoothly and dealt again. Abby arranged the cards in her hand and shook her head, apparently not too pleased with them. "I assume you want a card or three?" he asked.

Instead she gave him a sweet smile. "No, I'm okay."

He took two, which gave him two pair, but she beat him again, this time with three of a kind.

"I'll take your sweatshirt."

"You're not very subtle, Abby. You just want to look at my manly chest." He pulled off his sweatshirt and tossed it to her. "I hate to disappoint you, but as you can see, I still have a T-shirt on."

"Don't tell me you're *that* hot." Abby tossed the shirt back to him.

"Actually it's just getting warmer in here all the time, don't you think?" Back the shirt went to her.

They played another hand and he won. This time he demanded her sweater.

"And I hate to disappoint *you,* but I have a T-shirt on, too." Abby chortled as if he could actually see through the layer of wool. She was getting into the spirit of the game now.

"I'll win that next," he announced with a fresh surge of confidence. He dealt and, true to his prediction, won again and asked for her shirt. Abby flushed as though she actually had to remove it. She knew that what he was imagining was worse than actually undressing. He leaned forward and whispered,

"You've got such wonderful skin. So smooth and creamy. And your breasts are—"

"I've got a bra on," she said quickly. "An ugly bra. White cotton, very sensible."

"I have to say I'm disappointed. White cotton? Why, Angelina would never wear anything so practical. I remember how she used to describe the lace bikini panties she wore and the almost transparent nighties. I spent many a restless hour lying in bed, picturing her wearing those little scraps of nothing...and then taking them off...slowly...." He glanced over at her and was pleased to see the images he'd recreated had an effect on her, too. Her breathing was shallow and quick, and a telltale flush colored her cheeks.

Aware that this game was far more complex than mere poker, he gave them each more cards and did nothing to hide his delight when his luck held and he won the hand. "Okay. That takes care of the bra...ah, and it was worth the wait." He looked at Abby's still well-covered chest with an appreciative expression. "Hmm...nice. Just as I imagined, so soft and full." He flexed his fingers, cupping them as if her breasts were cradled in his palms. "They fit perfectly into my hands. Not too big, and certainly not too small."

"Shut up and deal." Abby's face grew pinker, and she crossed her arms over her breasts. But even with the protective shield of her arms and the three layers of clothing he could visualize her nipples hardening under his gaze.

They played several more hands until Abby in theory had lost all of her clothing, and Prescott was sitting in his jeans and undershorts. Abby was apparently finding it difficult not to stare at his chest, and he caught her attention riveted there several times. When he noisily cleared his throat, she swallowed hard and lifted her eyes to meet his amused gaze.

"Ready for bed now?" He put the cards into their box and tossed it onto the table. "I do believe I won this game. I'd like my winnings now, if you don't mind."

"Wha-what do you mean?" Abby edged farther away from him.

"Well, since it looks like you've got everything you won from me, it only seems fair that I should get what I have coming, doesn't it?" He held out his hand.

"No way, fella. You won every stitch I'm wearing."

"That's the way I remember it, too." He smiled and continued to hold out his hand as Abby just stared at him with her mouth open. "Shy, Angelina?"

"I—ah," Abby stuttered.

"Tell you what I'll do," he bargained. "I'll settle for a kiss. But it has to be good, not like the one you'd give an uncle with bad breath. A real kiss, Abby."

She took a shaky breath, moved closer to Prescott and placed her arms around his neck. For one long moment, they gazed into each other's eyes before he put his arms around her waist and pulled her against him.

Chapter Ten

He meant for the kiss to be light and teasing, but as soon as their lips touched, a blazing fire ignited deep within. Her fingers slid up his arms, now bare after the few poker hands he'd lost, and across the muscles bulging in his shoulders, then threaded themselves into the golden hair at the nape of his neck. She cupped the back of his head, encouraging him to continue.

As if she, too, felt flames of passion burning she melted against him. The softness of her body pressed against him from the firm curve of her breasts all the way down to the flat plane of her stomach. Her eagerness surprised and excited him.

But as his tongue traced the outline of her lips, he tasted the distinct flavor of vodka on her lips and was reminded how much alcohol they had consumed. He rarely drank except for a couple of beers with his men every once in a while. And from all he knew about Abby, she drank even less often. Sharing more than half a bottle of the Russians' finest vodka, especially on an empty stomach, was bound to have an effect on her.

Which meant that she was probably not entirely sober.

Which meant it would definitely not be gentlemanly to take advantage of her momentary weakness.

As much as he would enjoy the night, he would hate himself in the morning if she woke up and regretted anything that had happened. Abby wasn't a quick roll in the hay or, in this case, a cozy coupling on a Russian cot. She wasn't cheap and she wasn't easy. What a strange and unresolved situation. But she was his wife.

His body ached to be satisfied, but his honor wouldn't allow him to succumb to his desire. Never had it been such a difficult and yet such a clear-cut decision to pull away from her. With his hands firmly on her shoulders, he gently put some distance between them by holding her still while he stood.

"Prescott..." A disappointed moan escaped her still parted lips, and his resolve almost weakened. But even as he waged an internal battle, her eyelids drooped and she yawned. "I don't know what's wrong with me," she murmured. "I'm just so tired. I'll be okay in a minute and we can play another game." She giggled. "Maybe this time we could start out naked, and get dressed every time we lose a hand." A look of confusion crossed her face. "No, that wouldn't work. Then if you won every hand, I'd still be naked and you'd be—"

"Shhh," he said. "You had a little too much to drink. Get some sleep now."

She yawned again. "If I could just rest a minute..."

He helped her stretch out on the bed. Murmuring more sounds of protest, she burrowed her face into the limp pillow and rolled onto her side as soon as she lay down.

Prescott felt a rush of tenderness as he looked at her. Her dark hair billowed sinuously over the striped ticking of the pillow and provided a striking contrast to the smooth paleness of her complexion. Long black lashes rested against her cheeks and her delicious lips were curved into a smile.

"Sleep well, my love," he whispered and dropped another kiss on her forehead.

He sighed, wondering what would become of their marriage. She seemed determined to end it. At first he hadn't really cared because the whole marriage idea had been so spontaneous that it hadn't seemed real. However, once they'd gotten past that initial prickly stage, they'd settled into a comfortable relationship. But always, during the scientific discussions, the shared meals over the hot plate in their room or laughing at video movies in one of the recreation rooms, he was increasingly aware of an attraction toward her unlike anything he'd ever felt for any other woman.

Oh sure, Prescott had been sexually aware of many women's charms. But with Abby, it was more than sexual. He was almost as attracted to her intelligence and her subtle, dry sense of humor and the generosity of her spirit as he was to her body. *Almost*.

He unfastened her boots, tugged them off her feet and set them on the floor next to the cot. Her thick wool socks were damp, so he removed them, too. For just a moment, he cradled her slender feet before gently returning them to the bed. "You do have sexy feet, Angelina," he whispered.

His actions didn't wake her, but the chill of the room must have affected her feet because she wiggled her toes and shivered. Reluctant to stop looking at her, but beginning to feel the exhaustion of his hard day's work, Prescott unfolded the rough wool blanket lying on the end of the bed and spread it over her. In unconscious appreciation, she sighed and snuggled under the cover.

Not bothering to stifle his yawn, he added a few more logs to the wood stove and fashioned an impromptu bed out of two chairs. After removing his own boots, he made a pillow out of his sweatshirt, used his parka for a blanket, then turned off the lamp.

Outside, the muted sun persisted in sneaking around the heavy, room-darkening shutter that covered the single window in the small cabin. But it wasn't the light or the uncomfortable chairs that kept

Prescott awake long into the night, it was the woman sleeping peacefully on the bed.

ABIGAIL HAD NEVER BEEN so cold. The wind whipped snow into her eyes and shards of crystallized ice cut into her face. She tried to walk, but penguins flocked solidly around her feet, chirping and crying in their plaintive little voices. The stylishly feathered black birds surrounded her as far as she could see in all directions and completely blocked her progress.

"Lobo," she called, but her voice was snatched away by the wind and scattered over the white wilderness. She shivered and tried to pull her coat more tightly around her, but when she looked down, she was horrified to see that she wasn't wearing a coat. In fact, she was totally naked!

Abigail woke with a gasp and sat up on the narrow cot. It took her eyes a few seconds to adjust and her brain a few seconds longer to snap from the bad dream to the present. Still lingering on the fringes of the nightmare, she glanced down and was vastly relieved to see she was completely dressed except for her boots and socks.

Again she shivered, but this time it was from a very real chill in the air. Apparently the fire in the stove had gone out and the room temperature had dropped by at least twenty degrees. She wrapped the blanket more closely around her, but it did little to ward off the cold. Her nose felt numb and her fingers stiff. Then she became aware of Prescott trying to sleep on a couple of chairs. He shifted awkwardly on his makeshift bed and tried to snuggle under the parka, but it was obviously not big enough to provide an adequate cover.

Thoughts of last night's card game, followed by vague memories of some very heated kisses nudged their way back into Abigail's mind. Although she had a headache, which verified she'd drunk way too much, she remembered how irresistible Prescott had been and how much she'd wanted to make love with him. She also remembered feeling pangs of regret when he'd broken off the embrace and put her to bed. But she'd been too tired and too many drinks away from being sober to form any sort of effective protest.

Another wave of cold shook through her and she forced herself to get out of bed. Her socks were lying neatly across her boots, so she pulled them on before hurrying across the room to the woodpile. She was struggling with the mechanics of getting the chunks of hardwood to light when she heard the chairs scrape across the floor, followed by a muffled curse.

"Damn, and I thought sleeping on the ground was uncomfortable," Prescott muttered.

She glanced around as he approached and saw him massage his neck muscles, then flex his back. "You could have shared the bed with me."

He glanced dubiously at the narrow cot and gave her a crooked smile. "The only way we could have shared that bed is if one of us slept on top."

Their gazes locked and Abby felt her breath catch in her throat. That was exactly what she'd been wanting, and she wished, more than anything at the moment, that that was what he wanted, too.

"Having a little trouble with that?" he asked, and she managed to nod her response. He slipped his arms inside his parka and joined her to kneel in front of the stove. "With no trees on the entire continent, I can't help but wonder where the wood comes from," he commented.

Actually the thought hadn't occurred to her, but now that he'd mentioned it, she wondered, too. "Old ships?"

He turned the piece of wood over in his hands and studied its gray, weathered surface. "I suppose. It must be some sort of driftwood that washes up on the shoreline, because it sure didn't grow here."

In a matter of minutes, he had the fire blazing, but neither of them moved as the warmth began spreading into the room, chasing away the cold shadows. With the shutters still fastened across the window, the firelight bathed the couple in a rosy glow. A shiver that had nothing to do with the temperature raced down her spine as she became increasingly aware of his nearness.

"Did you say something?" Prescott held his hands toward the radiating heat.

"Not really. I was just shivering out loud, I guess."

"In that case..." He scooted closer, wrapped his arm around her shoulders and pulled her snugly against his side. With his other hand, he took both of hers and tucked them inside his parka against his bare chest. "Here, maybe this'll help."

He had no idea how much that helped, but not at all in the way it was intended. Yet as Abby looked up at him, she detected a flare of passion brightening his eyes that told her he was thinking of exactly the same thing.

"Abby, I—"

"Prescott, I—"

Both began to speak at the same time, then stopped, waiting for the other.

"I've never felt so close to you," she said, venturing to speak first. "And I don't mean just physically," she added to dispel any misinterpretations he might have made.

But he hadn't been confused about her meaning at all. "I know," he agreed softly. "Abby, this is just as I imagined it would be between us. I've dreamed of holding you and kissing you and..."

This time as his words drifted to silence, the eloquence of his gaze took over as it slowly caressed her face, lingering on her lips for several long seconds.

Like the needle of a compass being magnetically pulled to the north pole, she lifted her face and leaned toward him until she could feel the warm swirls of his breath against her mouth. She didn't know where the boldness was coming from, but she simply *had* to feel his lips against hers. It must be the mysterious Angelina finally showing up. She waited for the prudish

Abigail to speak up, but there was no sound in her ears except the rush of her own blood racing through her veins, pushed by the increased pounding of her heart.

As their lips touched, the tip of his tongue teased its way into her mouth, which she opened eagerly. His fingers threaded their way into the thickness of her hair as her own hands slid along his warm skin until they reached the muscular planes of his back.

Their bodies shifted until they were facing each other fully. Not that there was any space between them at this point. Their kiss deepened and seemed to suck the breath from her body. She could feel his hard, hot response surge quickly to an impressive size as it pressed into her tingling flesh. For the first time since they'd begun this field trip, she thought they both had way too many clothes on. Where was that deck of cards when she needed it?

Prescott must have echoed that opinion because his hands slipped down to the waistband of her pants, then under her sweater.

Abigail knew they were rapidly approaching the point of no return. If this was going to be stopped, she knew it had to be done immediately. But this desire for intimacy had been building between them for too long. Ever since that first polite, relatively impersonal message from Lobo, there had been a spark. When they'd actually met, that spark had turned into what she thought was hostility. But now she recognized it as animal magnetism, pure and simple.

His fingertips moved lightly across her skin, then up the bottom curve of her breast until they captured the pucker of her nipple. Her reaction was immediate and she felt herself swell beneath his gentle massage. His fingers burned into her skin even through the cup of her serviceable cotton bra.

He groaned, the sound swallowed by their unbroken kiss. When she didn't protest, he took the initiative to remove that barrier. His fingers fumbled with the clasp, signifying either that it wasn't something he'd done often enough to become adept at, or that he was as nervous as she was.

Abigail was in no mood to analyze her feelings or his motivations. All she knew was that she wanted to feel the sensation of his skin against hers . . . and his lips on her body.

They shifted slightly until he was able to stand from his kneeling position and pull her to her feet. Before she could take a step, he swept her into his arms and carried her the short distance to the narrow bed. Prescott shrugged out of his parka and it fell to the floor as he stretched out beside her. There wasn't much room, but with their bodies tucked so tightly together, there was no need for more space.

He returned to the task of freeing her breasts by lifting her sweater and T-shirt over her head. A rush of cold air left a trail of chill bumps on her skin and her nipples hardened into taut pink buds. He stared down at her, an approving smile curving his lips.

"You're even more beautiful than all my fantasies," he whispered.

"You fantasized about me?" Being the object of a man's fantasies was something she'd never thought possible for her.

"Abby, you have no idea how much sleep I lost because of you... both before *and* after we met."

She blinked in surprise, but before she could pursue the subject, his blond head lowered toward her breast. The tip of his tongue laved a wet trail around her nipple before he pulled it into his mouth. For a few seconds, his teeth gently teased her, nibbling and raking their slightly rough edges over her tender flesh. Just when she was ready to cry out in frustration, he began a rhythmic sucking that seemed to ignite every nerve ending in her entire body.

He pulled away just long enough to strip off the remainder of their several layers of clothing. He turned his attention to her other breast as he returned to her side and let his fingers begin a field trip of their own.

Sliding down to the softness between her legs, he unerringly found the center of her desire. Even though she arched against him, he refused to be hurried, but continued to caress a spot that was growing more sensitive by the second. As his finger slipped into her warmth, she moaned, aching to feel even more of him buried inside her.

His voice was ragged as he whispered her name over and over before recapturing her lips in a kiss filled with passion and anticipation.

"Yes..." she murmured, answering his unspoken question. "Yes, yes, yes..."

Her breasts flattened against his chest as he moved to lie on top of her. Centering between her legs, he eased into her. As he met a tightness, a resistance that proved her claim of virginity, he paused. Looking deeply into her eyes, a flurry of expressions crossed his features. "Abby?"

"Oh, yes," she repeated. To add further emphasis, she cupped his buttocks and pulled him deeper, through the barrier and into her body.

She held her breath, savoring every sensation of the moment. He, too, must have felt the magic because once he was as deep inside as he could go, he paused again. "You feel so good," he sighed. But as if he could wait no longer, he began moving with a natural cadence, gentle at first but with an increasing fervor that pushed them ever closer to the brink of abandon.

The aching throb of desire tightened within her until she could think of nothing else but relieving the sexual tension each thrust intensified. She didn't want to consider the problems they would have to deal with very soon, couldn't predict whether their marriage had a chance of success. She didn't want to think about the possibility that this would be the only time she would feel the heat of his body inside her or the passion of his kiss on her lips. There would be time enough to be logical and sensible and all those other emotions at which she excelled.

But for this one moment in time, she belonged here, in Antarctica, in a deserted Russian weather station, in the arms of the man she loved.

Yes, she loved him. She didn't know if she would ever have the confidence to say it out loud. Somehow by voicing such a deep emotion, she would be opening herself up to be hurt. Whatever the consequences of her rash, spur-of-the-moment decision, she would never regret being in this place with this man at this instant.

He thrust deeper, pushing away all thoughts except her need for fulfillment. The tension coiled tighter and tighter until it exploded with a force that caught her completely by surprise. She'd had her share of fantasies, too, but never had she imagined it would feel so wonderful. A dazzling display of fireworks danced across her closed eyelids while she floated weightlessly through time and space. These feelings defied all logic, all the scientific data she'd ever learned, all the laws of nature.

In a cloudy part of her consciousness, she was aware of Prescott's increased movements, followed by a long, shaky moan as he filled her with his heat. They clung together, holding on to the passion and the intimacy for as long as possible.

Slowly, Prescott relaxed on top of her, carefully supporting his weight so he didn't crush her. His face was buried in the curve of her neck as they waited for their heartbeats to slow to a more normal level. A drop of perspiration fell from his chest and trickled between her breasts before being stopped by stomachs still pressed damply together.

"I never thought I'd say this, but it sure is hot in here," she murmured, still barely capable of forming a coherent thought, much less carrying on a conversation.

"Do you want me to get up?" he asked, his voice muffled against her skin.

"No, this is..." As she searched for the right word, he finished the sentence for her.

"Perfect."

"Yes, perfect," she agreed.

"And as scientists we know how rare perfection is," he continued.

"Almost nonexistent," she agreed again.

"We should have taken notes." He lifted his head and looked into her eyes. "This is one formula I don't want to lose. Ever."

Once more, she agreed with him. But she kept quiet, not wanting any thoughts of tomorrow to intrude on today.

Chapter Eleven

"That was some Herbie, wasn't it?" the helicopter pilot shouted over the roar of the rotating blades. Prescott and Abby exchanged questioning looks and the pilot laughed. "That's what we call these sudden summer storms. Of course, they're nothing compared to the winter blizzards."

"Have you ever stayed all year?" Abby asked, wondering what type of personality it would take to withstand that type of climate.

"Me? Winter over?" He snorted. "No way. It'd drive me crazy. You should see these guys after a winter here. They're all pale and gray. And they jump at every little sound." The pilot shook his head. "I couldn't stand all that cold and darkness and silence."

They'd been in the air for only a few minutes, yet Abby's ears already hurt from the noise of the chopper. She could see how absolute quiet would be an extreme change for the man. Frankly, as much as she was thrilled with the chance to spend some time in Antarctica, the thought of staying for a whole year was a bit daunting. Especially right now when what she wanted more than anything in the whole world was a long, hot bath, a cup of steaming coffee and a big bed with clean sheets and lots of soft, snugly blankets on it.

And Prescott beside her.

As if reading her thoughts, he reached over and took her hand. They'd spent the whole morning in each other's arms, talking and making love. It wasn't until the radio call had interrupted to tell them the helicopter would be picking them up at sixteen hundred hours that they'd finally gotten dressed. They'd had to hurry to get everything put back as they'd found it, to repack their sled and to get to the pickup site on time. She hadn't had a chance to feel nervous about all that had happened between them.

Until now. The closer they got to McMurdo, the more anxious she became. Being in that cabin hadn't been reality. She and Prescott had been all alone in the world—Adam and Eve, surviving against nature. Through the forced togetherness, they'd formed a new bond. But back at the station, would their relationship continue to develop or go back to the way it'd been before they left?

And did it matter since she was scheduled to leave on a flight tomorrow?

That was the one subject neither had broached today. Abby wasn't sure if Prescott didn't ask because he was afraid to hear the answer, or because he didn't really care what the answer would be. He seemed to have accepted the fact that she had decided to leave early. Maybe he was even relieved. Maybe this morning had just been a sailor's holiday.

The helicopter hovered over the pad, then settled onto the marked frozen landing spot. The pilot shut off the engines, jotted a few notes in his log, then climbed out. He opened the door, but before he could react, Prescott had leapt out and was turning back to help Abby.

The breeze softly ruffled his blond hair, and she remembered how soft it had felt beneath her fingertips. Dark mirrored sunglasses hid his eyes, but she could still visualize what a bright shade of blue they were when he was deep in the throes of passion, or how tenderly they'd looked at her as they lay together on the narrow bed. And his lips... Ahh, she had so many memories of those lips and the way they'd felt on her body—*all* over her body.

Oh, how she loved him. And oh, how she wished he loved her enough to ask her to stay.

Prescott helped the pilot tie down the chopper, then they unloaded the sled and its contents. All three fell into step as they crossed the ice pack and headed toward the dormitories. They hadn't gone but a few feet when the roar of powerful jet engines split the air and a C-130 Hercules lifted off the runway on the other side of the station. It banked sharply overhead, then leveled out on a northerly course.

"Is that my plane?" Abby asked, knowing without hearing the answer that it was. There were only two scheduled flights a month.

The pilot didn't understand the significance of the question as he cheerfully answered, "If you were planning to be on that plane, you've missed it."

"But I thought it wasn't going to leave until tomorrow," she persisted.

He shrugged. "The weather's so unpredictable they leave when they can. Don't worry. He'll be back in a couple of weeks."

"A couple of weeks?" she echoed.

She glanced up at Prescott and saw he was watching her closely. There was no hint of his feelings in his expression, and she wished he would take off those damn sunglasses so she could see his eyes. No matter how much he tried to mask what he was feeling, they usually could be counted on to reveal his emotions.

But without any clue, Abby was left to respond on her own. She was secretly delighted to be given two more weeks without actually having to make any sort of decision. On the surface she was able to smile and say with studied nonchalance, "Oh, well, at least now I'll have time to help you do more work on the penguin study and finish my report on the hole in the ozone."

"I know how much you were looking forward to getting away from here," Prescott commented with equal casualness.

"I wouldn't say 'looking forward' exactly," she corrected. "It was more that I didn't feel there was a reason for me to stay."

"And now there is?"

She couldn't resist any longer. With trembling fingers that revealed just how important this conversation was, she removed his sunglasses. Before he could hide his surprise and shield his emotions, she saw exactly what she wanted to see. His eyes weren't the cool, icy blue that would have told her he didn't care. Instead they were warm and worried and just a tiny bit vulnerable as he waited for her final decision. She couldn't tell if it was love, but her heart skittered wildly at even the possibility that he held some lasting affection for her.

"Yes," she answered with a sigh of relief. "I think so."

His mouth curved into a wide, genuine smile. Before she even realized what he was doing, he pulled her into his arms and gave her a long, wonderful kiss. "Welcome home, Mrs. Roberts."

"So TELL ME ALL ABOUT IT," Sandy prompted as they sat in the galley, lingering over a second cup of coffee after lunch. "Was it really awful to have to spend the night out there alone?"

"Well, we weren't alone since there were two of us," Prescott informed her. "And it was a great adventure."

"An adventure, huh?" Sandy was skeptical. "Before coming here, the last time I had an adventure was when I was a teenager and we had to move during my senior year of high school. Did I ever tell you I was an army brat?" She laughed. "I said I'd never get involved with a man in the military, and just look at who I married."

"Maybe Bill will be stationed somewhere permanently," Abby suggested.

"Ha, that just doesn't happen." Sandy smiled with obvious affection. "When I signed on to work here, I'd just gotten out of a bad divorce and had vowed not to get involved in a romance for years. But as soon as I sat next to Bill on that transport plane, I was a goner."

"You mean you just met him on the trip here?"

"Yes, isn't that incredible? By the time we landed, we knew we were in love. The next day, we had a little private ceremony in the chapel. We even wrote our own vows."

"I guess I thought you two had known each other for a long time," Abby commented.

"It doesn't take a long time to know these things," Sandy assured her. "When it's right, it's right. But now I have to deal with the hassles of moving all over the country again. I never want to see another packing box in my life." She turned to Abby. "How many times have you moved?"

"Well, counting when I moved from my parents' house to my dorm room and then into my apartment—twice." Abby chuckled. "I guess I've never been a very mobile person."

"Ha! That'll change now," Sandy exclaimed. "I'll bet the captain won't be able to stay in one place for long. I think the travel bug gets in their blood, and they get bored if they're not in a new place every so many years. Either that, or they're born with wanderlust and go into the military because it keeps them on the move."

While Sandy chattered on about the joys and annoyances of moving so often, Prescott met Abby's gaze over Sandy's curly blond head. He wished he could read his wife's mind. What she was thinking at that moment?

Even though things had vastly improved since their night in the cabin, he still had no idea how committed she was to this marriage. Was it his imagination, or did she flinch every time someone mentioned their life together as husband and wife? Was it that distasteful to her?

Certainly, when they were alone in their room, there were no questions. They could barely keep their hands off each other long enough to undress and jump into bed. Never, in his wildest dreams would he have expected such passion and excitement. It was then that he was the most optimistic. Surely a woman who made love with such abandon and pleasure cared about her partner. Especially when that woman was Abby.

There were so many sides to her personality that he doubted he'd ever be bored with her. Her beauty was obvious and she seemed to have grown even more gorgeous in the past few weeks as her confidence built. But it was the woman inside that fascinated him. She was every inch a lady—intelligent, capable, well mannered. And yet when they were in bed together or in the shower or even once in the greenhouse where they'd met for lunch, she was a tigress. She could make him laugh and she could make him cry out in a passion so intense he sometimes thought he would pass out. It was an irresistible combination.

And he didn't want her to leave... ever.

But he didn't want her to stay unless it was her decision. Already he felt more than a little guilty because he'd gotten her here on a misunderstanding. Sure, she hadn't been absolutely truthful with him, either, but that didn't lessen his responsibility as a man to make wise decisions. It was just that time had run out, and he had hated the thought of being out of touch with her for four months. In a way, it had been selfish.

And even now, he had to admit to a degree of selfishness that he'd been very happy that she'd missed her plane last week. Watching the silver belly of that jet pass overhead had been one of the prettiest sights he'd ever seen. It meant they had two more weeks together—at least. Now it was up to him to convince her that she would be happier with him than without him.

"So what about Saturday night? You'll do it, won't you?" Sandy finished asking, then waited expectantly.

Apparently Abby hadn't been listening, either, because she gave a guilty shrug and a blank look when Prescott snapped back to the present. "Uh, sure, you can count on us," he improvised.

Sandy whipped a list out of her pocket. "Good, then you'll be team number twelve. Well, I'd better go. I'm trying to get at least twenty teams signed up. That's how many it'll take to make enough chili to go around." She tucked the list away and headed toward another group of unsuspecting victims.

"Chili? What's she talking about?" Abby asked.

As it dawned on him what they'd just agreed to do, Prescott began to laugh. "You won't believe it, but we've just entered a chili cooking contest."

"Excuse me, did I hear you correctly? Does that mean you and I are supposed to *cook*?"

"Yeah, pretty funny, huh?"

"And people, our friends and co-workers, are supposed to *eat* this stuff and survive?"

Prescott nodded. "Do you think we should use our Russian canned-meat recipe?"

"I don't think the world is ready for that yet," Abby retorted.

Prescott sobered when he realized she wasn't as amused at the situation as he was. "How difficult can it be to cook chili? All it takes is meat, beans and some hot stuff."

"But I can't cook," she argued. "You *know* that."

"Don't worry about it. We can fake our way through it."

"We don't even have a recipe. I think we need to be a little more exact than 'some hot stuff.'"

"Surely you have an old family recipe for chili lying around somewhere."

Abby threw up her hands in despair. "My family never cooked chili. In fact, I can't remember eating it except at Mexican restaurants."

He could see this was really upsetting her, and he wanted to find out the real reason. Tenderly he hooked his forefinger under her chin and lifted her head, forcing her to meet his eyes. "What's wrong, Abby? It's not just the chili, is it?" To his dismay, her dark blue eyes filled with tears. "Sweetie, tell me, please," he cajoled.

"It's silly," she said, trying to pull away and hide her feelings.

But he wouldn't let the matter drop. Instead he pulled her to her feet. "Let's go to our quarters and talk about this."

She protested, but went with him. After they were seated on opposite corners of the bed, he prompted her again. "Now tell me what's wrong. And nothing is too silly, Abby."

She looked uncomfortable, but she said, "It's embarrassing."

That admission took him by surprise. "What is?"

"I'm a grown woman—and your wife. It's embarrassing that I can't cook. And now everyone will know."

He stared at her in relief. "Oh, sweetie, that's no problem. I'm no cordon bleu chef, but I can throw together some decent meals. I'll be there to do most of the cooking. All you have to do is slice, dice and stir."

When she still seemed to be upset, he moved closer and pulled her onto his lap. Cuddling her against his chest, he nuzzled his face into the sweet-smelling curls of her hair. "You are so talented and wonderful and beautiful. It doesn't matter to me that you can't cook. If you want to learn, you can. If not, we'll get along okay with our hot plate." She didn't say anything, but he could tell she was listening. "Besides, I have a confession to make," he added.

"What?" She leaned back and looked up at him.

"I can't fix a car. I know, it's a man's job to work on cars. But I don't like to fool with them. I've never changed a spark plug or the oil or anything. Not even changed a tire."

A shaky chuckle softened her lips. "I've changed a tire before...once. Maybe we're a better match than we thought."

Prescott looked into her eyes and he was overwhelmed with the strength of his feelings for this woman. "Abby, I wanted to tell you—"

A pounding on the door interrupted him and scattered his thoughts. "Captain Roberts, there's an urgent call for you in your office, Sir," the young lieutenant said when Prescott opened the door.

"I'll be right there." He gave Abby an apologetic smile. "We'll finish this conversation later."

But later was even later than he thought. There had been a breach of security in one of their confidential areas, and Prescott didn't make it back to their room until two o'clock in the morning. He quietly let himself in and didn't even bother with a shower, but undressed and climbed into bed.

Even though Abby was sleeping soundly, she shifted until her body was snuggled up against his. With her back against his chest, his arms wrapped around her and his face nestled comfortably against her hair, he sighed. He'd never experienced such supreme satisfaction as when he held his Angelina in his arms.

It was then that it dawned on him with a clarity that shook him to his very soul. He loved Abby. He'd fallen in love with her personality over the computer, and now he'd fallen in love with the woman. And he would tell her as soon as the time was right. He didn't want to just blurt it out in the heat of passion. So far he hadn't timed this relationship too well. Even though he'd already told her on the computer that he loved her, that had been between those other two people—the wild and crazy sides of their personalities. Now that he'd fallen in love with the whole woman, he wanted this declaration to be unquestionable. Maybe it wouldn't make any difference to her and she would fly off into the wild blue yonder as she'd planned. But at least she wouldn't leave without knowing how he felt.

THE DAY FOR THE CHILI cookoff turned out to be warm—by Antarctic standards. The thermostat hovered just above freezing. A mixed feeling of anticipation and dread filled Abby as she forced her sleep-drugged eyes open to face the new morning.

As had become his pattern in the past few days, Prescott had already gone. Even though they'd slept together for almost a month and a half, most of that time without anything but the most accidental of physical contacts, Abby missed having him next to her when she awoke. It was amazing how quickly she'd become accustomed to having his warm body pressed against hers or waking to see how young and handsome his face looked as he slept.

And at the moment, Abby wished he was with her to calm her nerves about the upcoming contest. She knew she had overreacted. But the thought of displaying her inadequacy in public terrified her. She'd never had any self-confidence about her looks or her domestic skills, only her work and her education.

Her mother had been a wonderful housekeeper. She'd always cooked elaborate meals for her family. And she'd spent hours in the kitchen baking pies and other delicious pastries. Because there had been no real need to learn or any encouragement from her mother, Abby had avoided the kitchen. While her lack of culinary ability was sometimes inconvenient now that she was grown, it had never actually been an embarrassment. Until she'd fallen in love with Prescott.

It was a new type of pressure. Not only did she want him to think she was intelligent and capable, but she wanted him to think she was sexy and desirable. And she wanted him to believe she would make an excellent wife—for him.

And as she'd admitted at least this part of her concern, she'd been touched by his reaction. He'd been so sweet and understanding. After apologizing for getting them both into such an unlikely situation, he'd promised to do most of the work. The night before, they'd spent the entire evening searching through old magazines in the lounge areas for chili recipes.

They hadn't found one that was for just plain chili, but they'd collected enough variations that they figured they could pool all the ingredients and come up with some sort of edible facsimile.

But as the deadline approached for the judging, Abby paced the room nervously. Where was he? What was taking him so long? He'd promised to be back in plenty of time.

When a knock resounded through the room, she knew it was bad news. A baby-faced ensign passed on the unwelcome message that the captain couldn't get away yet, but that he would meet her in the galley. And worst of all, he said for her to start without him.

Grumbling under her breath, she gathered the pages of recipes, bundled into her usual outdoor gear and headed toward the mess hall. When she arrived, all the other teams were already hard at work, preparing their ingredients and stirring the bubbling contents of their pots.

"Hi, Abby. I was beginning to wonder if you'd changed your mind," Sandy said as she hurried toward her.

"I think it's safe to say I still feel exactly the same about the contest since I first heard about it." Abby was instantly sorry for her cranky tone and tried to temper it with a smile. "So where do I pick up my ingredients?"

"Kevin will help you." Sandy's curls sprang around her head like corkscrews as she looked around the room. "I've got to check on everyone's progress. Let me know if you need anything else."

Abby walked into the storage room with growing trepidation. Where *was* Prescott?

"Yo, Miz Roberts. What's cookin'?" Kevin, the cook's assistant, chortled at his little pun.

"Nothing yet," she answered. "That's why I'm here to see you."

"What can I get ya?"

She shuffled through her recipes, then shrugged. "Oh, everything that's usually in chili. Especially a lot of those green things." She glanced at the piles of vegetables and spices he had waiting.

"You mean the peppers?"

"Are they hot?"

"Very hot."

Abby nodded. "Yes, that's what I want. Oh, and throw in a few of those little red ones, too." He gave her a nervous look, but complied. "And Kevin, can you give me any hints? You know, secrets of the trade?"

"Now, Miz Roberts, you know I can't do that. Why, that'd be cheatin'," he responded in his Georgia drawl.

"Okay, but will you pretend that I've given you a list and you can just give me whatever is usually included in chili." She turned the full force of her blue eyes on him, testing her newly discovered feminine wiles. And she was truly amazed when they worked like a charm.

"Yes, ma'am. I'll do that." Kevin picked up a small box and began loading supplies into it. "But you have to figure out how to put it together by yourself."

"Yeah, sure, leave me the hard part," she muttered under her breath. "Prescott, where are you? If you don't—"

Kevin finished filling the box with ingredients and a large pot. "Here ya go, ma'am. Everything you could possibly need."

Abby poked around in the box and pulled out a bag of beans. "I thought these things came in cans."

"Sorry, no canned stuff allowed. All contest entries have to be made from scratch. There are all kinds of spices out there on the table, so use whatever you need." He glanced at the large clock on the kitchen wall. "You'd better get started, though. The beans take quite awhile to cook." He grinned at her, then went back to his work before she could pry any more cooking information out of him.

Abby eyed the beans. They weren't very big. How could they possibly take *awhile* to cook? But she supposed it was all relative. Maybe it was quite awhile when compared to boiling water or cutting up the vegetables. She peered into the box at the remainder of its contents. There were several fresh tomatoes, probably from the greenhouse since that was one of the few vegetables being successfully grown on the station, some onions and peppers, and a chunk of frozen meat. She shook her head and sighed. "Well, I guess I'd better get at it. Prescott, wherever you are, you'd better have a darn good excuse for being late."

Looking cautiously around, she noted that everyone was dumping all their ingredients into their one assigned pot. Assuming it couldn't be all that difficult if everything was cooked together, Abby felt encouraged. Maybe she could bluff her way through this ordeal.

Delicious smells competed with each other in the large kitchen as she chopped up every item that Kevin had included in the box. She scraped everything off the cutting board and into the pot, then wrinkled her nose at the pile. It didn't look right. Surely it needed some sort of liquid.

She cast a surreptitious glance at the contestant beside her and saw she was pouring water into her pot. Okay, that made sense. Abby carried the pot to the water jug and filled it about half full. She stopped at the table long enough to sprinkle a generous amount of every spice available into her mixture, then she returned it to her assigned burner. After stirring it and settling the lid on top, she turned on the burner and stood back to wait.

"Is that a secret recipe?" Carol Ann asked.

"Very secret," Abby answered wryly. No one but Prescott would know just how secret.

Carol Ann lifted the lid and sniffed. Her eyes were filled with tears as she said, "It sure smells . . . hot."

"That's just the way Prescott likes it," Abby informed her. And even if it wasn't, he was going to have to eat some just to keep her from killing him for leaving her all alone after getting them into the contest.

The door to the kitchen burst open and Prescott came striding in with Penny waddling right at his heels. "Abby, I'm so sorry. I just couldn't—"

She held up her hands. "Don't explain. Just help me think of reasons for the judges *not* to taste *our* chili. I doubt that a court-martial for murder by poison would do your career any good."

"Now, sweetie, it can't possibly be *that* bad. After all, we had all those recipes—"

"I didn't use them. I sort of glanced at them, but it would have taken me forever to measure all those things and—"

"You mean, you didn't measure anything?"

"Well, no. Kevin loaded it all in a box, so I figured it should all go in."

Prescott cautiously lifted the lid as if expecting the contents to explode. As soon as a cloud of spicy steam hit his face, his eyes watered and he turned his head quickly as he sneezed. "Lots of peppers, huh?"

"Didn't you tell me that chili is supposed to be really hot?"

"Yes, but—"

"Okay, this chili's *really* hot." She gave him an angelic smile. "And you're going to love it, aren't you?"

"I'm sure of it." He gave her an affectionately crooked grin. "Anything your pretty little hands have touched has got to be good."

"Kissing up to me at this point won't do you any good," she admonished. "Your name is already mud because you were so late."

"You took the first shift, so I'll do the rest."

She accepted his offer without argument, and promptly left the overheated room. "Let's get out of here, Penny, before someone is tempted to add you to their chili," she offered with uncharacteristic generosity to the small annoying creature.

Penny looked up at her adored Prescott, then echoed his sneeze. As if deciding that there was some wisdom in Abby's suggestion, the bird rubbed her beak against his leg, then followed Abby outside. "Okay, you can run along now," Abby said when Penny stopped and looked up at her expectantly. "Look, just because you think Prescott's your father doesn't make me your mother. What you need is a male in your life."

"Honey," Diane commented, "that's what we all need."

Abby opened her mouth to protest that she certainly had never needed a male. But she realized that while she might not actually *need* him, she *wanted* him. And it felt good to have a man in her life, however temporarily.

Chapter Twelve

The judges moved down the line of numbered bowls. They stopped at each, tasted its contents, jotted down notes on their scorecards, ate crackers and drank some ale or water to clear their palates, then moved on to the next.

Abby stood next to Prescott and watched with growing concern as the judges approached their bowl. "Did you taste it?" she whispered to him.

"No, did you?"

She shook her head. "I wouldn't know good chili if I tasted it. Besides, I'm not that brave."

He gave her a wink. "We're in this together, babe. If I go to the brig, so do you."

"Thanks a lot." But she couldn't keep from smiling. Prescott had the knack for making her see the humor in every situation. He made her recognize that she'd taken life too seriously for too long.

The judges stopped at entry twelve and ladled spoonfuls onto their plates. With clean plastic spoons, they took a taste. For a second no one moved, then simultaneously they all reached for their glasses.

"A little too much chili pepper maybe?" Prescott whispered to Abby. "Or was it jalapeños?"

She shrugged. "My lips are sealed."

The judges refilled their glasses and downed more gulps of cooling liquid before taking the time to write on their scorecards. They continued taking sips of their beverages as they walked to the next entry.

"I think that's a good sign, don't you?" Abby asked.

"What?"

"The fact that they ate it and were able to walk away."

Prescott's laughter rumbled through his chest. "You're too hard on yourself. Before long, you'll be baking bread and stuffing turkeys and all sorts of things."

"Ha! Not me!" Abby protested vigorously. "That's your job. I'm going to take auto mechanics and repair cars, remember?"

He wrapped his arm around her shoulders and pulled her against him. "You're incredible."

The judges finished their duties, then met in a corner to compare notes. It only took them a couple of minutes to reach a decision and one of them held the ribbons while the spokesman went to the microphone. "Okay, everyone, here are the results of the annual chili cookoff contest." He consulted his scorecard and cleared his throat. "We had a lot of excellent entries this year, and a few that were...well, interesting. And the winner this year is entry number three."

Sandy shrieked and Bill swept her into his arms for a congratulatory hug. She looked so cute in her frilly apron and with her short blond hair fluffed into bouncy curls that perfectly matched her personality. She was the very image of a happy homemaker, and Abby felt a pang of envy because she could never truly see herself in that role.

One of the other judges handed Sandy the blue ribbon and a reporter for the local newspaper, *The Antarctica Sun Times*, snapped pictures of Sandy and Bill accepting their prize.

"And this year we've added a new category." The judge took a drink of water and dabbed at his eyes with a handkerchief. "Usually we give the red ribbon for the second-place entry. But this year, we're creating a new category. For the hottest chili, and, folks, I do mean *hottest*—I'm from Texas so I know hot when I taste it—the winner is entry number twelve."

Abby didn't know whether to laugh or cry. But Prescott set the tone by bowing low and saying, "My wife and I thank you and sincerely hope there's a good supply of antacids in the clinic. Oh, and I will take it personally if each and every one of my men don't sample my chili."

"Prescott!" Abby hissed.

"It'll grow hair on their chests," he responded. His gaze slid down the front of her red sweater and he leaned over to whisper in her ear, "Don't you dare eat any. I don't want anything to mar the beauty of your chest."

That now-familiar curl of desire tightened inside her and Abby's eyelashes dropped in unconscious seduction. There was just something about Prescott that brought out her femininity.

There was a semiorganized surge toward the food with some people starting toward the salad bar and others heading straight for the chili.

Abby did dare to taste her chili but managed only a little bit on the tip of her tongue before she had to put out the fire with a gulp of cold water. She couldn't help but notice the teary reaction of Prescott's men as they cheerfully choked down a respectable portion. In fact, it became a macho challenge to see who could eat the most, and Abby and Prescott's chili was the first to disappear. Luckily there was plenty of beer to wash it all down, so by the end of the meal everyone was feeling pretty mellow.

Bill jumped up on the platform at the end of the room and took over the microphone. "Now that everyone's full and semidrunk, I think it's time for our talent show. I know there are lots of strange, I mean talented, people here at McMurdo. So, who's going to be first?"

A group of secretaries volunteered and stripped down to leotards to perform a song-and-dance number from *A Chorus Line*. Abby sipped a glass of wine and sat next to Prescott at a table near the front with Diane and her date, Jim, and Sandy and Bill.

The next act was a comedy skit done by some of the young male and female naval officers that had everyone rolling in the aisles. It did a lot to lift Abby's spirits until the next singer came on stage and warbled out a Garth Brooks imitation of "Somewhere Other than the Night." That song referred to a long-married couple rediscovering love, and it reminded Abby that her own marriage might not last until Christmas. No amount of wishing and hoping would keep it together if Prescott didn't love her.

But the conversation at their table was lively and hilarious, and she couldn't stay sad long. Abby soon relaxed and had a terrific time. With Prescott's arm draped possessively across the back of her chair, she loved being part of a couple. The other two couples had had more traditional beginnings to their relationships than she and Prescott had. But, for the first time, Abby began to fantasize about how it would feel if she and Prescott *did* manage to stay together.

Several other acts followed, all different and all entertaining. As the evening progressed, Abby was increasingly amazed at the quality of the performances. Already she'd realized there was a true cross section of people here at the station. No matter what sort of service was needed, from someone to do acrylic nails to someone who could paint murals to someone who could repair the much-coveted television sets, there was a person capable of handling the job. Usually these favors were handled on an exchange basis, which intensified Abby's feelings of inadequacy since she felt she had no special skills. The only thing she could offer was her ability to reprogram a computer. But once her talent for computers had become known, she'd spent quite a few evenings loading video games on all the station's computers—for off-hours use, of course.

A wild quartet finished their version of a Mötley Crue song that left the older members of the audience rubbing their ears and the younger members clapping enthusiastically. Bill left the table and returned to the stage to introduce the next act. "Now, folks, we have a real surprise. It's not common knowledge, but our own Captain Roberts is an accomplished saxophonist." There were some surprised murmurs from the audience, including a gasp from Prescott himself. "I'm sure we can persuade him to perform for us," Bill continued. "Everyone give the captain a big hand and maybe he'll bring that sexy sax onstage."

One of the navy men in the crowd jumped to his feet and yelled, "Yo, Captain, way to go. Give us some Kenny G."

Another voice called out, "Look out Bill Clinton!" More cheers followed until it was a roar he couldn't refuse.

"You never told me you could play the sax," Abby whispered in shock.

He gave her a sheepish smile. "The subject never came up, and I didn't want to toot my own horn...so to speak."

He gave her hand a quick squeeze, then succumbed to the encouragement of the audience. "I'd love to play, but I left my sax—"

"I just happened to have stopped by your office and picked it up for you," Bill interrupted, taking away Prescott's last excuse.

The crowd applauded as Prescott took the stage and Bill handed him his sax case. The captain stepped up to the microphone and smiled at the audience. "No Kenny G tonight," he said, then raised his hand to silence the responding moans. "I want to play something special for my bride."

He opened the case, took out the shiny brass instrument and fastened the strap around his neck. He raised the saxophone to his lips and looked directly at Abby. After blowing a few practice notes, he launched into a mellow version of Billy Joel's "Just the Way You Are." Even though no words were being sung, the lyrics danced through Abby's mind, pulled along by the touching melody.

At the end of the song, tears were running freely down Abby's face as the crowd stood to cheer and demand an encore. Prescott shook his head. "No, I'll give someone else a chance to embarrass themselves," he said with a laugh.

"How about you, Abby?" Bill asked from the stage. "Surely you have some sort of talent you'd like to share with us."

Abby hesitated, and Prescott hurried to take the microphone from Bill. "Now don't put my bride on the spot like that," he said, clearly defending her from what he saw as a potentially humiliating situation. Obviously he hadn't believed her computer-generated story about being a musician, either.

But that was one thing she hadn't stretched the truth about. With a confident smile, she stood and walked over to the stage. "May I borrow your sax, sir?" she asked, giving Prescott a wink.

"Sure, but you don't have to—"

"Thanks," she said, and took the instrument from his hands. After wetting her lips and the reed, she lifted the instrument to her lips. Prescott's shocked gaze was still focused on Abby as the soulful, heart-rending music of Nat King Cole's "I Apologize" began pouring from the horn. When the song ended, the room was silent for several seconds, then everyone burst into wild applause.

"Hey, she plays better than you do, sir," one of Prescott's men joked.

"Maybe *she* should run for president," someone else commented.

But onstage, Abby's and Prescott's gazes remained locked. Her vision was blurred with tears as he gently took the sax away from her and replaced it in the case. Then, tenderly, he opened his arms to her.

Without hesitation, Abby stepped into them and nestled her head against his chest. His fingers reached up to stroke her silky hair, and he rocked her gently from side to side.

"I mean it, Prescott," she said softly. "From the bottom of my heart, I apologize."

"So do I, Abby," he murmured. With his arm still around her, he led her offstage and into the appreciative crowd.

"Now that's what I call an apology," Sandy said to no one in particular. "I wonder what they had to apologize for."

But Abby and Prescott knew.

This touching moment effectively ended the talent show. It was late and everyone began clustering in small groups as they gathered their possessions and talked about plans for their day off tomorrow. Prescott's arm stayed around Abby's waist, and they were heading toward the door when it burst open and the station's communications clerk burst in. "I have an emergency message from the States."

A hush fell over the audience. It was the kind of news everyone dreaded. While tucked away in the self-contained cocoon of McMurdo, it was easy to pretend the rest of the world didn't exist. Time off the Ice seemed to stand still. So when news of a death or serious illness reached the station's inhabitants, it struck a double blow. The time factor was usually critical. Either it was already too late or by the time the person returned home, nothing could be done, anyway. Sadly, there often could be no last good-byes.

The messenger's gaze searched the group, and everyone held their breath while hoping he wouldn't call their name. Finally he found who he was looking for and walked forward, not stopping until he was in front of Bill. "Congratulations, sir," the clerk said with a wide smile. "You're a father!"

"But the b-baby's not due for th-three more months," Bill stuttered.

"Your wife went into labor early, but she and the babies are all fine."

"*Babies?*" Bill echoed.

"She had twins, sir, two boys. And she needs you to come home right away."

There was a collective gasp, and everyone turned to look at Bill, including Sandy. From the stricken look on her face, it was obvious she hadn't known he had a wife. "You mean *ex*-wife, don't you?" she asked in a weak, shaky voice.

From the strained expression on his face, the answer was clear even before he shook his head. "I'm sorry, Sandy. I meant to tell you, but we were both lonely and..." He shrugged. "You knew this was just temporary. It's been fun, but—"

"*It's been fun!*" she shrieked. "I thought you loved me. What about our wedding ceremony?"

He shrugged. "I didn't mean to hurt you. A lot of people have Ice marriages."

Sandy's face grew even more pale and she swayed as if she was about to faint. "And what about *my* baby—*our* baby?" Her voice was so soft that only those closest to her heard the question.

By the way Bill's eyes widened, it was evident he heard. "You—you told me you were taking the Pill," he stammered. "I have two—no, four kids back home. I didn't want any more."

This was the final straw. In a show of strength that seemed to surprise even her, Sandy's hand whipped out and slapped Bill hard across his handsome face, so hard that he staggered a few steps back from the blow.

"Sandy, I—"

But she didn't wait to hear more. Whirling around, she pushed past Abby and Prescott and stumbled toward the door.

Abby didn't hesitate as she looked up at Prescott and said, "I've got to go with her. She's in no condition to be alone right now."

He nodded, and she hurried to catch up with Sandy in the entryway. Sandy had already run outside without stopping to put on her coat or boots. Abby hesitated just long enough to grab her coat off the hook. Struggling to put it on, she ran after her friend. "Sandy," she called. But the blonde didn't slow down until she reached her room in the dormitory. Her fingers were shaking so badly and she was crying so hard that it took her a few seconds to realize she'd left her keys in the pocket of the coat she'd worn to the mess hall. In complete defeat, she sank to the floor.

Abby sat down beside her and pulled the woman into her arms. Even though they were about the same height, Sandy collapsed against Abby, leaning into her and seeming much smaller. "I'm really sorry," Abby murmured, feeling woefully inadequate to handle the woman's tears. "I thought the two of you were perfect for each other."

"So...did...I," Sandy choked out. "It was love at...first sight. I thought...it would...last forever."

"Things may still work out."

Sandy shook her head emphatically. "No, it can't now. I didn't know about his wife. I honestly thought he loved only me. But now that I know that I was just a temporary fling—an Ice wife—how could I ever trust him again?"

"Then maybe you're better off without him. You have to think about your child and start making plans for both of your futures."

Sandy rubbed her hand across her forehead. "I've got to go home. I just can't think here. Nothing's real. Nothing's normal. No one's who they say they are, and things aren't as they seem." She took a deep, shaky breath. "Things are different here because we can pretend to be anyone we want to be. But once it's over, it's over. We go back to who we were before and all this is like a bad dream."

Abby tried to think of something to refute that. But the more she thought about it, the more she realized how profound Sandy's statement was. And she and Prescott were a perfect example of that. She wasn't as outgoing, witty or attractive in real life as she'd felt since her arrival at McMurdo. But here, they were playing their roles. He was the dashing naval captain and she the adventuresome scientist. Back in Boulder, those descriptions wouldn't apply at all.

Diane came running down the hall with Sandy's coat and boots. Together she and Abby unlocked the door and helped the distraught woman into her room. They undressed her, pulled a clean nightgown over her head and tucked her into bed. "I'll stay here with her tonight, just in case," Diane offered.

"No, that's okay," Abby said. "I've got some heavy thinking to do, and I don't mind sitting with her. Would you tell Prescott for me?"

Diane hesitated, but when Abby settled onto a rocking chair near the bed, she gave in. "Okay, but just call if you need anything."

"I will. Good night." Abby didn't mean to sound abrupt, but once a thought process had begun, she wanted to pursue it without interruption. She managed to keep smiling until Diane had wished her a good-night and closed the door behind her.

As she looked around the room, she realized that Bill's belonging's were everywhere. She knew he would be back for them at any time, so she dumped all his things into the duffel bags in the closet with his name on them, then left them outside the door and locked it tightly. What Sandy didn't need right now was another confrontation with Bill—especially if she didn't want complications with her baby.

And what Abby needed right now was some time away from Prescott so she could think clearly.

Sandy was right about a lot of things. It was definitely a different world here. Everyone had told Abby that people seldom kept up friendships once they returned home. There was something critical that didn't survive the transfer. Perhaps the key factor was that while people were on the Ice, they had everything in common. They ate the same thing at the same time and usually in the same place as everyone else. Except for minor variations, everyone's room looked the same. Everyone worked the same hours and had very little opportunity to expand their individuality. Everyone even dressed alike in the clothing they'd been issued.

But once they returned home, they could become individuals again, with their own tastes and interests. They now had choices, and those choices often didn't coincide with those of their friends from McMurdo.

Abby shivered as cold fingers of premonition tightened around her throat, making her gasp for breath. She and Prescott hadn't been attracted to each other in the real world. What made her think they would be when they returned to it? They would quickly grow bored with each other.

How could she have possibly thought it would work? So what if Prescott had dedicated that lovely song to her tonight? He'd never actually told her he loved her except on the computer. Why should she believe he would still be interested in her once they were back in Boulder?

That is, if he even decided to return. What if she was just his Ice wife and he had no intention of extending their marriage beyond his tour of duty here? When she considered the circumstances of his proposal and the ratio of men to women at the station, it all made perfect sense. He simply hadn't wanted to be stuck on the Ice without someone to warm his bed for four long, lonely months. Sure, he could have found a woman at McMurdo, even several. But by bringing his own woman with him, he had more control over the situation and could send her home if the liaison cooled.

Abby felt the tears trickling down her cheeks, and she knew what Sandy must have been feeling when she realized Bill wasn't her knight in shining armor and that her life wasn't as perfect as it seemed to be.

The Ice was a fantasy world, and it was time for a return ticket to reality. One way.

Chapter Thirteen

Prescott squinted sleepily at the clock when he heard the door open, then click shut. It was almost six in the morning. He would have to get up for work in a few minutes, and he'd been hoping to have a little time to hold Abby in his arms before leaving. Actually, last night he'd felt like they were on the verge of something special and he'd been very disappointed that they hadn't had a chance to talk. And, of course, after the talk, he'd hoped to seal this new phase of their relationship with a night of passionate lovemaking.

And now they would have just a brief chance to say their good mornings before he had to leave for the office. More than likely she would want to get a few hours of sleep before going to the lab. He rolled over and sat up, his gaze searching the darkened room for Abby. When he couldn't immediately discern her in the shadows, he reached for the lamp.

"Oh, I'm sorry, I didn't mean to wake you," she said as the light filled the small room.

"That's okay. I tossed and turned all night, wondering what was going on with Sandy and Bill."

"There's no more Sandy *and* Bill. He's a creep, and she's heartbroken." Abby got down on her knees and pulled out her suitcase from under the bed, placed it on the top and opened it. "A plane is on its way here now. It'll have a short turnaround so it can leave at noon."

Prescott rubbed his fingers across his eyes. "Are you letting Sandy use your suitcase?"

Abby walked to her dresser and pulled open one of the drawers. Scooping her underwear into her arms, she carried it to the bed and dumped it into the suitcase. She was returning for a second load when she finally answered his question. "No, I'm not lending it to Sandy. I'm using it myself."

"What?" She was depositing another armload of clothes into the suitcase, and turning away again when he reached out and grabbed her arm to stop her. "Abby, what's going on?" he demanded. "Look at me and tell me what you're doing."

Slowly, as if it was the most painful thing in the world, she lifted her gaze to his. "Both Bill and Sandy are flying home today. But not together—"

"Dammit, I don't care about Bill and Sandy." Prescott didn't realize his fingers had tightened on her arm until she grimaced. Apologetically he relaxed his grip, but not enough to completely release her. "I'm talking about you...us."

Abby didn't blink as she said, "I'm going to be on that plane, too."

If she'd hit him in his stomach with her fist, he couldn't have been more surprised. For a moment, he was absolutely speechless. He felt as if all the air had whooshed out of his lungs. "But—but I thought you'd changed your mind," he finally managed to say.

Her expression softened and she sighed. But just as he thought she was going to stop her foolishness, she straightened her shoulders and her eyes grew cold. "I knew from the beginning that this was a mistake. I tried to pretend it would work, but face it, *Bert,* this whole idea was crazy."

He released his hold and pulled his hand away, letting her arm drop to her side. Obviously, last night hadn't been quite the milestone he'd thought it was. He felt his own jaw tighten in a reaction to her tone and her attitude. Even her choice of words caught him by surprise. She hadn't called him Bert in over a month. And somehow, reverting to the usage of that old name canceled out everything that had happened in between.

She hesitated and her fingers opened then shut as if she was restraining herself from something. Then she whirled around and went back to the task of transferring her clothes from the drawers to the suitcase, except that now her movements were jerkier and more frantic.

Prescott decided he didn't need to sit there and watch his whole life fall apart. As casually as he did it every day, he tossed back the covers and strolled naked to his dresser. He picked up the underclothes he needed, then selected a uniform from the wardrobe and, without a glance in her direction, walked into the bathroom.

He deliberately took his time shaving and getting dressed. It wasn't so much to allow her time to leave, but to give him a chance to try to think things through. Usually his logical, analytical mind could sort right through problems, no matter how big or small, and find the solution. Or if there was no clear solution, he took steps to make certain the problem wouldn't reoccur.

In this case, his logic deserted him. Thoughts and memories and dreams all swirled together until he couldn't distinguish one from the other. At what point had his fantasy ended and reality begun? When had Abby been Abigail and when had she been Angelina? They were actually three different personalities. He'd lusted after the fantasy, been annoyed by the stone-faced professional in the lab coat, and fallen in love with the quick-witted, intelligent, sexy lady he'd gotten to know on the Ice. Or thought he'd gotten to know.

Apparently he didn't know her at all.

By the time he left the bathroom, dressed and outwardly prepared for the day ahead, she was already gone. As he looked around the room that oddly seemed so much smaller without her, his heart constricted into a tight knot. He realized he'd been hoping against hope that she'd still be there, waiting to talk this out. But obviously their relationship wasn't important enough to discuss... or salvage.

As further evidence that she was putting the whole episode behind her, she'd left her velvet wedding dress on the bed. Lying on top was a brief note. "Drop this on the skua pile. Maybe someone else will want to use it for their Ice wedding."

But even more painful was the sight of her wedding ring lying on his pillow. As far as he knew, it had never been off her finger since he'd put it on. Even when they'd gone through their darkest times together, neither had taken off their rings. He picked it up and dropped it into the small corner tray in his sock drawer.

He skipped breakfast and went straight to his office, settling for a cup of coffee because he knew his stomach wouldn't tolerate solid food right then. After snapping at his clerk, then apologizing three times in a row, Prescott shut himself inside his office and tried to bury himself in his work. He'd discovered the source of the breach of security and even the person involved. Now all he needed to find was a motive. Unable to uncover a logical reason for taking the risk, he was temporarily baffled.

And even though he usually didn't listen to music at work, he dropped a tape into his cassette player and turned it on. Loud. Loud enough to drown out the sound of jet engines as Abby's plane lifted off the Ice and headed toward New Zealand, and out of his life.

ABBY COULDN'T RESIST looking down as the plane ascended into the sky. It was odd, because from up here the continent seemed to be a plain, uniform shade of endless white with just a few patches of frozen earth and rocks beginning to show through in the early summer thaw. But the appearance of the landscape from up here was deceiving. She knew from her field trips with Prescott, when they'd studied and photographed the icebergs, that they were as individual in their size, shape and coloration as the people that made up McMurdo Station. At first she'd thought the vivid blues of the sky were reflected in the crystal depths of the ice, but on closer examination she and Prescott had discovered that myriad jeweled tones, from the palest touch of emerald green to the deepest shades of sapphire blue, were within the ice itself. These floating islands of ice had a depth and beauty often missed by the insensitive eye.

She thought with regret of the trip they wouldn't get to make to the Dry Lakes to search for fossils. Her journey to Antarctica had been more of an experience in learning about people than in learning about the history of the continent as she'd planned.

Instead of studying scientific theories that completely excluded the human factor, Abby had been thrust into a situation of confinement and forced intimacy, not only with the man who was her husband, but with strangers who had become her friends. She'd spent more time worrying about them than concentrating on her research, which for Abigail Harris was highly uncharacteristic.

Her month and a half at McMurdo was something she'd never forget or regret. Leaving Prescott had been the most difficult thing she'd ever done. But she truly believed it was better for her to leave him now than for him to leave her later. With every passing day, she'd fallen more deeply in love with him. So it was only logical that it would hurt less now than later.

Logical, a voice inside her head scoffed. *Sometimes you're too logical for your own good. Here's where you end up by listening to your head and not your heart.*

But Abby closed her mind to that inner voice. Obviously her heart didn't make wise decisions, so she had better start using her head once more.

"I'm so glad you're here with me," Sandy whispered as she leaned toward Abby and clenched her arm. "I would've hated having to travel just with *him.*"

Her tone left no doubt to whom she was referring even if Bill hadn't been the only other passenger on the plane. He sat several rows back, studiously avoiding making any sort of eye contact with the two women. In fact, he seemed more worried about the possible consequences of his early return on his career than either his wife in the States or his Ice wife.

"Have the two of you talked any more about the baby and his responsibilities to it?" Abby asked.

"No." Sandy's eyes filled with tears. "I can't...not now. I thought I might go back home and stay with my sister for a while until I figure out what I'm going to do."

"This is too big an issue just to let drop," Abby advised. "You're going to have to face him about it sooner or later."

Even as she spoke the words, Abby recognized the irony of her advice. She hadn't exactly sat down and talked to Prescott about her fears and feelings. She realized she'd done exactly what she'd told Sandy not to do—she'd run away to avoid facing her own problems. It was easier to leave than to stay and risk being hurt.

But she salved her conscience with the knowledge that she'd left him a note. He'd find it when the moment was right. And maybe he would understand. Again, she was struck by the irony. She wasn't sure even she understood what had happened . . . or what never would.

PRESCOTT TAPPED his pencil on the metal edge of his In basket. It was still piled high with reports he couldn't deal with because he simply couldn't concentrate. In spite of everything, he'd heard the plane pass overhead, and his thoughts followed Abby as she flew north, rapidly putting miles between them.

"Let it go," he chided himself. And he truly intended to succeed. It was just a matter of time before he erased all thoughts of *that* woman from his mind.

He punched the On button of his computer and watched as the program booted up. On the screen it was noted that he had a message on his daily calendar. Since that was where he or his clerk usually left meeting reminders and other scheduled appointments, Prescott called it up, hoping it wasn't something too critical. He sure would hate to be responsible for making a critical decision today. His brain wasn't exactly functioning at its optimum level right now.

The computer cycled through until the note was displayed on the screen. His eyes skimmed it and his heart pounded as he read the words again more slowly.

Dearest Lobo, Prescott and Bert,

I couldn't leave without telling you how I feel about us, but I couldn't seem to find the words when we were in the room together. Since writing you on the computer has always been easier, I thought I'd say my goodbyes this way.

I blamed you for not being truthful, but I know that it was as much my fault as yours. Just as I am now hiding behind this computer screen to pour out my feelings, you and I were both taken by the anonymity of being pen pals. Perhaps the reality was a disappointment for you, but I wanted to tell you that the man I got to know while on the Ice was the most wonderful, exciting person I've ever met. He was definitely the kind of man I'd like to spend the rest of my life with.

Unfortunately, you and I won't be at Mc-Murdo forever. Soon we'd be back in the real world, trying to adjust. And, dear Lobo, my greatest fear was that we couldn't make the transition. I can't tell you how much I loved waking up with you each morning. But someday I knew I'd wake up and not see that love in your eyes or even worse, see resentment or boredom when you looked at me, and I'd be crushed. It's easier for me to leave now before the sun sets so the memories we have of each other will always be good ones.

I've decided not to go back to BioGen, but to find a new job somewhere else. Just send whatever paperwork is necessary for the divorce or annulment to my post-office box. I'll keep it open indefinitely.

I wish you the best of luck with your life and your career. Thanks for including me in a small part of it.

I love you,
Abby

Prescott's chair groaned in protest as he leaned back and studied the screen for several minutes. She loved him. And he loved her, although apparently she didn't know that. But for some misguided reason, she seemed convinced that the romance wouldn't last anywhere except in the fantasyland of Antarctica.

Why would she think that? He shook his head. Sure, things were different here. People let their hair down and explored the different sides of their personalities that they'd never dared expose before for fear of rejection. There was a freedom here unlike anything most people had felt because they knew that in five months it would all be over and they'd probably never see any of those people again.

Abby must have felt that freedom. But she must also have been very aware of the time limitation. She needed security and reassurance, and all he'd offered her was a vacation on the Ice.

He should have told her he loved her. He should have spent more time making plans for their future, talking about the kinds of things married people usually discussed, such as kids and a house and saving for a vacation.

When Sandy and Bill's "marriage" had fallen apart, Abby must have seen her own marriage as being in the same danger. She doubted his commitment and feared he would do the same thing to her. And since Abby didn't have the experience in relationships or the confidence about herself as a desirable woman, she'd left rather than wait for him to end it.

Prescott stood and yanked his parka off the hook by the door. Well, dammit, she was wrong. He loved her and he wanted her in his life forever. He should have been more sensitive and noticed her insecurities. Now he had to find her and convince her that this wasn't a marriage of convenience, but a "till death do us part" kind of commitment.

But was it too late? There wouldn't be another plane for at least two weeks. By then, she'd be back in the States and probably relocated. Every minute counted, but here he was, stuck a thousand miles from nowhere with no means of transportation.

Restlessly he walked to the airfield with Penny dogging his heels, chattering her displeasure at his lack of attention. The wind was brisk off Winter Quarters Bay, but Prescott barely noticed as he stood at the edge of the Ross Ice Shelf and looked out to sea. Several hundred yards offshore, a Russian trawler sputtered along, its nets down. Prescott immediately recognized it as the boat he and Abby had seen when they'd been tagging the penguins. Just as it had been doing then, it was fishing. The crew was probably planning to sell the day's catch to one of the stations on the Ice to satisfy the need for fresh seafood on its menu. Or maybe the vessel was there to pick something up. A message perhaps? Or a package? Or information obtained by someone who'd violated security?

He straightened as the pieces of the puzzle began fitting together. That trawler could provide the answers to several questions.

ABBY LOOKED DOWN at the return ticket in her hand. She'd missed her flight . . . again. Well, she hadn't actually missed her flights. She'd just decided not to make them. And for a person who had never even been late for a dental appointment, missing even one flight was a phenomenon.

When the military transport had landed seven days ago, it had been her intention to jump on the first flight home. But the magic of New Zealand had beckoned her, so she decided to be a tourist for a few days, since it was unlikely she'd ever get down here again.

So she'd seen Sandy off on a flight to the United States, then rented a car and driven all over the small country, from the heights of Mount Cook, across the rich green fields dotted with thousands of sheep, to the sparkling beaches of the coastline. She'd been surprised to discover it was a lot like Colorado, but with a certain charm she found fascinating.

When it came time for her second flight, she'd overslept after staying out all night walking along one of those beaches and enjoying the beauty of the moon and the stars. It was incredible how much she'd missed nighttime. The depth of a dark sky with its nightly display of celestial bodies was something she'd always taken for granted.

And somehow, even though she and Prescott had never shared the romance of a full moon or sparkling stars except across the impersonal impulses of the computer line, she couldn't look at the night sky without thinking of him.

Actually that wasn't the whole truth. It wasn't just at night that she thought of Prescott—it was every moment of every day. Whether she was awake or asleep, he was there, inside her mind, inside her heart.

She tossed the ticket onto her dresser. Tomorrow. She would definitely leave tomorrow. It was time she finished this chapter in her life. But how could she when she would never again be with the man she loved?

The salty sea breeze lifted her hair and swirled it around her face as she stepped outside. Abby pushed it back and held it out of her eyes as she gazed out to sea. Because her hair was so thick and curly, she'd always worn it pulled back into a tame ponytail or twisted on top of her head. But since her adventure with Lobo, she'd let her hair down. Funny, that was exactly the cliché she'd used to describe the people at McMurdo. And she was the guiltiest of all.

Had she truly been herself while she was there?

She'd spent a lot of time thinking about that in the past week as she toured the countryside. The very ambivalent answer she'd come up with for that question was yes . . . and no. The Abby who'd made wild, passionate love to Prescott was certainly not a part of who she'd been before. But it was a part of her nonetheless. The scientific, serious Abigail who'd respected Bert's intelligence, but who'd been too shy to explore any sort of relationship was her. The sensuous, teasing Angelina who'd had such fun flirting with Lobo was her. And the Abby who desperately and deeply loved Prescott was her.

If she could be three distinct personalities and yet still be capable of loving just one man, why couldn't Prescott? He'd adapted to his surroundings just as she had. Maybe she hadn't given them a chance to make it. Maybe her fear of being hurt and rejected had caused her to overreact. Maybe they could have had a long, happy marriage.

If only he loved her.

Now she would never know. Not unless she was to see him again. If only they could sit together somewhere normal and just talk. But it was too late. She'd turned in her Antarctic gear. They probably wouldn't consider allowing her to return. Other than CompuLink she had no way of getting in touch with him, and even then he'd be off-line until he returned to the States in March or April.

Abby sighed and leaned back against a large lamppost. Overhead, gulls squawked and swooped, searching for food along the wharf. It was a busy place, especially this time of year with everyone out of school and off work for vacations. People walked along the docks, shopping or stopping for lunch while others spent their time on the boats, preparing for a day of sailing or fishing. Accents from every nation reached her ears and the pungent, distinctive scents of the sea filled her nostrils. And all the while the only thing she could think of was how much fun it would be if Prescott was here with her.

A shabby Russian trawler caught her attention and she watched it nudge its way toward the dock. Abby knew next to nothing about boats, but she could have sworn it looked familiar. But then she'd spent so much time here at the docks in the past couple of days that it was no wonder she might think she'd seen it before.

Abby was turning away when she thought she heard someone call her name. She glanced around, but all she saw was a sea of strangers' faces, laughing and having a wonderful time with their loved ones. She started walking when she heard it again.

"Abby!"

This time she studied the crowd, but still didn't see anyone she recognized. Besides, what were the odds that someone she knew would be here, in Christchurch.

"Angelina!"

This time it was unmistakable. Abby stood on tiptoe, searching for the beloved face of the only person who had ever called her that. "Prescott?"

He broke through the crowd and walked toward her. For a second, she thought she must be dreaming. Seeing him was what she wanted most, but expected least at that moment. "Abby..." He stopped about a foot in front of her and stared down at her as if he was as shocked to see her as she was to see him.

"But what—why...?" Abby's words faltered.

"I can't believe you're still here."

"I'm leaving tomorrow."

He reached out and, with one large hand, cradled her cheek. "Please don't go." It was the next best thing she wanted to hear. When she didn't respond, he took a step closer until their bodies were almost touching. "We need to talk, Abby," he continued. "For all the words we've written or said, there are many things we've never discussed."

"Such as?"

"Such as—" he looked into her eyes and there was no hint of teasing "—I love you, Abby. I may not have used the best judgment in the way that I asked you to marry me, but I was very serious when I said my vows. And I'm very serious now. This is not just an Ice marriage or a reason for me to get you into bed. I want this marriage to work."

"Oh, Prescott, so do I," she cried and threw her arms around his neck. Their lips met in a kiss filled with love, passion and relief. "I was so afraid...." She leaned back and sniffed. "What's that smell?" she asked, aware that the odors of the wharf had suddenly grown much stronger.

"Uh, that's me," he admitted, and glanced down at his dirty clothes. "It was the only way I could get here without waiting for the plane. And I didn't want any time to be lost. I was afraid I'd never catch up to you before it was too late."

"You came all the way from Antarctica on *that?*" Abby looked at the shabby craft with horror.

"Seven *long* days and nights," Prescott verified. "The smell of fish has permeated into the wood of that boat. I don't think I'll ever eat seafood again."

"It could have been worse. They could have given you canned mystery meat." For the first time in a week, she felt her face relax into a smile at the sound of his laughter.

"But I did uncover some interesting equipment hidden behind all the bait and nets," he added. "It seems that harmless-looking Russian trawler is transporting scientific information from McMurdo to whoever will pay the highest price. But enough about that. Most importantly, it provided transportation to get me to you." Again he pulled her into his arms. "Abby, promise me you won't ever leave me again."

She shook her head, loving the feel of his chest beneath her cheek even if he did smell like an aquarium gone bad. "I've waited for you all my life, Prescott." He kissed her again with such passion that her knees threatened to buckle. "I think we'd better go to my hotel room before we become the center of attention here," she said. "Besides, I think you could use a nice, long bath."

His eyes twinkled. "Only if you'll take one with me."

"After all that water rationing we had to do at McMurdo, my first bath here was like a luxury."

"Cleanliness is *not* my primary goal," he admitted with a sexy wink. They looped their arms around each other's waist and started walking away from the dock. "And later we can talk about how many kids we want—"

"Kids?" she echoed.

"Oh, and I was thinking that the Dry Lakes might be the perfect place for our long overdue honeymoon."

"Looking for fossils?" she asked.

He stopped in the middle of the street and gave her another deep kiss. "Maybe, after we've made love for about five days. After all," he added, "they've been there for millions of years, so they're not going anywhere. But you and I have only about seventy years left to be together."

And neither Abigail, Angelina nor Abby could argue with that logic.

HARLEQUIN®

AMERICAN ◆ ROMANCE®

You asked for it...and now you've got it. More MEN!

MORE THAN MEN

We're thrilled to bring you another special edition of the popular MORE THAN MEN series.

Like those who have come before him, Sean Seaward is more than tall, dark and handsome. All of these men have extraordinary powers that make them "more than men." But whether they are able to grant you three wishes or to live forever, make no mistake—their greatest, most extraordinary power is that of seduction.

So make a date next month with Sean Seaward in
#538 KISSED BY THE SEA
by Rebecca Flanders

MILLION DOLLAR SWEEPSTAKES (III)

No purchase necessary. To enter the sweepstakes and receive the Free Books and Surprise Gift, follow the directions published and complete and mail your "Win A Fortune" Game Card. If not taking advantage of the book and gift offer or if the "Win A Fortune" Game Card is missing, you may enter by hand-printing your name and address on a 3" X 5" card and mailing it (limit: one entry per envelope) via First Class Mail to: Million Dollar Sweepstakes (III) "Win A Fortune" Game, P.O. Box 1867, Buffalo, NY 14269-1867, or Million Dollar Sweepstakes (III) "Win A Fortune" Game, P.O. Box 609, Fort Erie, Ontario L2A 5X3. When your entry is received, you will be assigned sweepstakes numbers. To be eligible entries must be received no later than March 31, 1996. No liability is assumed for printing errors or lost, late or misdirected entries. Odds of winning are determined by the number of eligible entries distributed and received.

Sweepstakes open to residents of the U.S. (except Puerto Rico), Canada, Europe and Taiwan who are 18 years of age or older. All applicable laws and regulations apply. Sweepstakes offer void wherever prohibited by law. Values of all prizes are in U.S.currency. This sweepstakes is presented by Torstar Corp., its subsidiaries and affiliates, in conjunction with book, merchandise and/or product offerings. For a copy of the official rules governing this sweepstakes offer, send a self-addressed, stamped envelope (WA residents need not affix return postage) to: MILLION DOLLAR SWEEPSTAKES (III) Rules, P.O. Box 4573, Blair, NE 68009, USA.

SWP-H494

HARLEQUIN®

Weddings, Inc.

WEDDING INVITATION
Marisa Carroll

Brent Powell is marrying Jacqui Bertrand, and the whole town of Eternity is in on the plans. This is to be the first wedding orchestrated by the newly formed community co-op, Weddings, Inc., and no detail is being overlooked.

Except perhaps a couple of trivialities. The bride is no longer speaking to the groom, his mother is less than thrilled with her, and her kids want nothing to do with *him*.

WEDDING INVITATION, available in June from Superromance, is the first book in Harlequin's exciting new cross-line series, **WEDDINGS, INC.** Be sure to look for the second book, **EXPECTATIONS**, by Shannon Waverly (Harlequin Romance #3319), coming in July.

American Romance is goin' to the chapel...with three soon–to–be–wed couples. Only thing is, saying "I do" is the farthest thing from their minds!

You're cordially invited to join us for three months of veils and vows. Don't miss any of the nuptials in

May 1994   #533 THE EIGHT-SECOND WEDDING by Anne McAllister
June 1994   #537 THE KIDNAPPED BRIDE by Charlotte Maclay
July 1994   #541 VEGAS VOWS by Linda Randall Wisdom

GTC

This June, Harlequin invites you to a wedding of

Promised Brides

Celebrate the joy and romance of weddings past with PROMISED BRIDES—a collection of original historical short stories, written by three best-selling historical authors:

The Wedding of the Century—MARY JO PUTNEY
Jesse's Wife—KRISTIN JAMES
The Handfast—JULIE TETEL

Three unforgettable heroines, three award-winning authors! PROMISED BRIDES is available in June wherever Harlequin Books are sold.

HARLEQUIN®

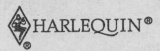

HARLEQUIN®

Don't miss these Harlequin favorites by some of our most
distinguished authors!
And now, you can receive a discount by ordering two or more titles!

HT #25551	THE OTHER WOMAN by Candace Schuler	$2.99	☐
HT #25539	FOOLS RUSH IN by Vicki Lewis Thompson	$2.99	☐
HP #11550	THE GOLDEN GREEK by Sally Wentworth	$2.89	☐
HP #11603	PAST ALL REASON by Kay Thorpe	$2.99	☐
HR #03228	MEANT FOR EACH OTHER by Rebecca Winters	$2.89	☐
HR #03268	THE BAD PENNY by Susan Fox	$2.99	☐
HS #70532	TOUCH THE DAWN by Karen Young	$3.39	☐
HS #70540	FOR THE LOVE OF IVY by Barbara Kaye	$3.39	☐
HI #22177	MINDGAME by Laura Pender	$2.79	☐
HI #22214	TO DIE FOR by M.J. Rodgers	$2.89	☐
HAR #16421	HAPPY NEW YEAR, DARLING		☐
	by Margaret St. George	$3.29	
HAR #16507	THE UNEXPECTED GROOM by Muriel Jensen	$3.50	☐
HH #28774	SPINDRIFT by Miranda Jarrett	$3.99	☐
HH #28782	SWEET SENSATIONS by Julie Tetel	$3.99	☐

Harlequin Promotional Titles

#83259	UNTAMED MAVERICK HEARTS	$4.99	☐
	(Short-story collection featuring Heather Graham Pozzessere, Patricia Potter, Joan Johnston)		

(limited quantities available on certain titles)

	AMOUNT	$
DEDUCT:	**10% DISCOUNT FOR 2+ BOOKS**	$
	POSTAGE & HANDLING	$
	($1.00 for one book, 50¢ for each additional)	
	APPLICABLE TAXES*	$ _____
	TOTAL PAYABLE	$ _____
	(check or money order—please do not send cash)	

To order, complete this form and send it, along with a check or money order for the
total above, payable to Harlequin Books, to: **In the U.S.:** 3010 Walden Avenue,
P.O. Box 9047, Buffalo, NY 14269-9047; **In Canada:** P.O. Box 613, Fort Erie, Ontario,
L2A 5X3.

Name: _____

Address: _____ City: _____

State/Prov.: _____ Zip/Postal Code: _____

*New York residents remit applicable sales taxes.
 Canadian residents remit applicable GST and provincial taxes.

HBACK-AJ